"Aren't you going to draw a line down the middle of the room and tell me to stay on my own side?"

Grant couldn't stop the grin that curved his lips.

Katie glared at him. The man knew exactly when to turn that smile on. Just when she'd worked up a good head of steam, he turned off her heat. Well, he could grin until his face split open. He was not sleeping with her in that...that... She couldn't find the word, but it certainly wasn't *bed*. Not with that glass roof and all those windows and the sound of the ocean crashing against the rocks at the bottom of the rocky ledge.

Scandalous! That's what it was.

An aphrodisiac.

A blatant enticement to make love.

And, heaven help her, she wanted to....

Dear Reader,

Having planned weddings for two daughters, I'm convinced that they operate on the premise of Murphy's Law—if it can go wrong, it will. And for me, it did: invitations had the wrong date, the bride gained weight and her gown didn't fit, the groom's tux would have held him and the best man, simultaneously, and too many more crises to count.

When I was thinking about the plot for my next American Romance novel, my daughters' weddings came to mind, and I wondered what would happen if the ultimate disaster came into being. What if the bride discovered she was already married, but *not* to her groom?

In *The Overnight Groom* Katie Donovan and Grant Waverly find themselves in just such a situation. Their sometimes catastrophic, sometimes funny, all the time loving journey to a solution will teach them that true love, even when it's put on hold for seven years, cannot be denied.

So, with a wink and a smile, I'm requesting the honor of your presence at the *next* wedding of Katie and Grant. The bride and groom promise this will be the last time they get married, because this time, it's for good!

Blessings to all my readers,

Elizabeth Sinclair

The Overnight Groom

ELIZABETH SINCLAIR

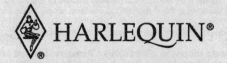

HARLEQUIN®

TORONTO • NEW YORK • LONDON
AMSTERDAM • PARIS • SYDNEY • HAMBURG
STOCKHOLM • ATHENS • TOKYO • MILAN • MADRID
PRAGUE • WARSAW • BUDAPEST • AUCKLAND

ISBN 0-373-16787-3

THE OVERNIGHT GROOM

Visit us at www.romance.net

Printed in U.S.A.

ABOUT THE AUTHOR

Elizabeth Sinclair was born and raised in the scenic
Hudson Valley of New York State. In 1988 she and
her husband moved to their present home in St.
Augustine, Florida, where she began pursuing her
writing career in earnest. Her first novel reached #2
on the Waldenbooks bestseller list in the second week
of its release and won a 1995 Georgia Romance
Writers' Maggie Award for Excellence.

As a proud member of five RWA affiliated chapters,
Elizabeth has taught creative writing and given
seminars and workshops at both local and national
levels on romance writing in general, how to get
published, chapter promotion of published authors,
writing a love scene and writing the dreaded
synopsis.

Books by Elizabeth Sinclair

HARLEQUIN AMERICAN ROMANCE
677—EIGHT MEN AND A LADY

Don't miss any of our special offers. Write to us at the
following address for information on our newest releases.

Harlequin Reader Service
U.S.: 3010 Walden Ave., P.O. Box 1325, Buffalo, NY 14269
Canadian: P.O. Box 609, Fort Erie, On t. L2A 5X3

To Anita. Without your generous help I never would have done your beautiful state justice. Thank you, dear friend, for sharing Maine with me.

And, always, to Bob, who gives me love, support and understanding, even when supper's late and the house looks like who-did-it-and-ran. I love you.

Chapter One

Married? Me? Grant Waverly, the perennial bachelor?

As shock waves that would have jammed the Richter scale rumbled through his body, Grant struggled to keep his lower jaw from hitting his chest. A joke. It had to be a joke. Vocal chords paralyzed, he gazed at the other lawyers around the rectangular, boardroom table. Their somber faces stared back at him.

Good grief! They're serious!

"Is there some reason you felt it necessary to leave us in the dark about Mrs. Waverly?"

He could hear Alfred Biddle, his boss, but for the life of him, Grant could not force a sound past his lips in answer. Instead, he nodded dumbly, trying to fight off the feeling that he'd just stepped into a parallel universe.

A faint snicker started at the end of the long, polished table, then swelled until the room filled with laughter. Grant glanced around the table, his gaze coming to rest on the slender, white-haired man at his right. Alfred's lips curled slowly into a smile.

"Well, my boy. No harm done. Mind you, we are a bit put out that you kept this a secret, but considering what an asset you are to the firm…"

"Asset?" *Was that croak my voice?* Grant wondered.

"Besides, the office rule is that we don't discuss personal matters on company time, but you really should have included it in your résumé under personal data." Alfred brushed an imaginary bit of lint from his immaculate suit jacket sleeve, then chuckled. "And I guess marriage could be classified as personal."

The seven senior lawyers laughed.

"Personal?" What had happened to his voice? He pulled at the perfectly executed knot of his navy, silk tie.

Dignified laughter broke out anew around the table.

"I can see we took him by surprise." Daniel Hoffman, the second in command at Biddle, Hoffman and Henderson, Miami's second most prestigious law firm, smiled first at Grant, then Alfred. "I've never seen Grant speechless before. Is this the same man who argued Anderson, Sheffield and Somes's best man into the ground in a courtroom just a few weeks ago?"

Again, everyone laughed. Everyone, but Grant. He was still busy trying to find his real voice to tell them that this was all a very bad mistake. He was *not* married.

He squirmed. His tailored gray suit suddenly felt like a suit of armor. Throwing caution to the wind, he opened his mouth, but Alfred stopped all conversation with his raised hand.

Daniel Hoffman patted his arm. "This new bit of information will certainly enhance your chances of filling the junior partnership opening up next month. You have no idea how close you came to being overlooked. But your marriage puts a whole new slant on things." He leaned closer to Grant and lowered his voice to a conspiratorial whisper. "Around here we like our top men to be happily married."

The other six senior partners nodded sagely, affirming Daniel's statement.

"Junior partnership?" Grant cleared his throat. He was beginning to sound like a parrot with a bad cold. "Me?"

"We're jumping the gun just a bit here, Grant. The appointment isn't to be announced for a while yet, and there are other candidates. But, when I say that your prospects are looking very promising, I don't think I'm being too premature." Alfred gathered the government security report spread out before him, straightened the pile of papers, then shoved it all into the manila folder his blond secretary handed him.

"But, sir—"

"No need for modesty," Alfred interjected. "We're all aware of the way you've been burning the midnight oil since you came here eight months ago. Then, of course, there's the Sampson contract you negotiated last month. The kind of results you got for one of our top clients on that contract says a lot for your expertise, young man." He cleared his throat, as if the compliment had left him dry. Then he stood. "I think it's time we took Grant out so the rest of the office can congratulate him and the other candidates on making the list."

Everyone agreed, stood and then moved in one body toward the boardroom doors. Everyone but Grant. He wasn't at all sure his legs would hold him. Learning he was supposedly married and eligible for a junior partnership in less than sixty seconds took some getting used to. He could get used to the partnership. After all, he'd worked hard enough to be noticed by the senior members of the firm. But this marriage thing was playing hell with his equilibrium.

"Come along, Grant. Get your due." Alfred beckoned from the doorway.

"Be right there, sir." Grant hung back. His mind whirled like an out-of-control child's top.

His due. Thinking about marriage and "his due" in the same sentence sent a chill racing down Grant's spine. Only once, in college, had he come close to popping the question, but his views on the importance of his career had clashed with those of the lady in question, and they'd gone their separate ways.

Since then, he'd sat in too many bars, with too many friends, drinking too many martinis over their divorce papers not to shudder at the thought of Grant Waverly ending up the same way. As a result, he'd studiously avoided the Holy State of Insanity. At least, he thought he had.

He shook himself. This was crazy. Of course he wasn't married. Surely he'd remember an event like that. There had to be an answer. He could find it. He just had to think for a while.

Daniel had said that when the government did the security check on the firm's employees, they'd discovered his marital status. If the government could find such information, surely Ray, his ace paralegal, could find it again.

He smacked the tabletop. Of course. Now it was beginning to make sense. The government had made mistakes before. His supposed marriage was nothing more than another of their classic screwups, like the draft papers they'd sent his aunt's Pomeranian. They'd probably confused him with another Grant Waverly. How many times had the IRS audited some poor soul, only to discover they had the wrong person?

He should have no problem proving this marriage business was all a case of mistaken identity. Then what?

He glanced at the closed boardroom door.

What about the junior partnership? He'd worked long and hard to get where he was, giving up a social life and using his expensive apartment like a motel room. Now, the first step on the ladder to senior partner dangled within his reach and a screwup by the FBI might just snatch it away as quickly as it had come.

"Grant?"

Rousing himself, he sprang from the chair and strode toward Alfred, who hovered with his head and shoulders just inside the door. "Coming."

Opening the door wider, Alfred stepped inside. "You okay, my boy?"

Grant nodded. "Fine. Just thinking."

"About running home to the little woman with the news, I'll bet." Alfred slung an arm around Grant's shoulders. "Well, come on outside and take your bow, then you can hurry home to the wife."

Wife.

Swallowing hard on the word and the lie he was about to perpetuate, Grant followed Alfred through the door. Grant's foot had barely cleared the sill when the applause broke out and people started slapping him on the back. Outwardly, he acknowledged their congratulations with a big smile and a firm handshake. Inwardly, he began processing the possible places he could crawl into and never be seen again.

"RAY, GET IN HERE. I need your help." Without waiting for the man to answer, Grant hung up the phone, swiveled the leather chair to face his office door and waited for his paralegal to arrive.

Ray would know what to do. If it could be found, Ray could find it. He knew every nook and cranny of the legal world and could gain access to any computer system known to man. As unconventional as he was, Ray Kozlowski was the firm's greatest legal research asset.

A few minutes later, a tall, good-looking man with a congenial smile, a shock of uncombed brown hair and a T-shirt reading Wolverines! Go Blue! concealed beneath his rumpled sport jacket entered the room.

"You rang, boss?" Ray pulled an Oreo out of his coat pocket, then munched thoughtfully.

Foregoing his usual lecture on the importance of office decorum, good grooming and obedience to the office dress code, Grant ushered Ray to the computer on a side desk. Fairly shoving the man in the chair, Grant pointed at the keyboard.

"Find out if I'm married."

"Excuse me?" The half-eaten cookie hovered inches from Ray's lips.

Impatiently, Grant explained his predicament. "You remember that government contract we're negotiating for Sam Putnam?" Ray nodded. "Well, the Pentagon insists that anyone working on a military contract with a high security rating has to be checked out from birth. Since I'm part of that team, they did a check on me and found that I'm married. Or at least, they say I'm married. I say it's a mistake."

"Geez." Ray's eyes grew big. He took another bite of his cookie.

Grant ignored the crumbs that tumbled to the freshly vacuumed carpeting.

"That's not the half of it. The senior partners were so pleased to find this out that they're offering me a junior partnership. Marriage is one of the prerequisites."

"Double geez," the paralegal mumbled around a mouthful of cookie.

"Before I break the news to them that it's a mistake, I have to pinpoint the problem. That's where you come in. I need you to work your magic and find out who this Grant Waverly is that they're talking about."

"Ah...boss, I need to know a few things. Like where the crime took place and the name of the other victim."

Grant shrugged and began to pace the length of the plush burgundy carpet. "Hell, if I knew that, I could check this out myself with a few well-placed phone calls."

"Okay. Keep your shorts on. Let me think." Ray stared as if mesmerized at the blank screen, drumming one set of his fingertips on the polished wood desk, while the other retrieved another Oreo from his pocket. He began to mumble. "The problem is that there's no central computer bank holding the information on marriages. Marriage records are kept in the city where they're performed...." His voice trailed off in thought. "You sure you don't remember where you got married?"

"Dammit! I've never been married!" Why was everyone so eager to put a noose around his neck?

Ray eyed him for a moment. "Never?"

Shaking his head, Grant straightened the brass nameplate on the edge of his desk. "The closest I ever came was a staged marriage in college."

Ray stopped drumming his fingers and swung to face Grant. "Didn't you go to a college somewhere in New England? We can check all the towns around there."

Grant shook his head. "That's not where the ceremony took place. A bunch of us from the college flew to Las Vegas for a long weekend during spring break. We met this so-called *minister* in a bar and, after a few drinks, we talked him into performing a fake ceremony. The guy got his license out of the back of *Field and Stream.* The marriage was never recorded.'' No need to tell Ray how much he'd wanted it to be the real thing at the time.

The paralegal went back into his thinking mode. Grant waited, trying to control his impatience.

"Well," Ray finally announced, swinging back to the keyboard, "I'm not sure this will work, but let's start with the marriage capital of the world—Las Vegas, Nevada.''

As Ray's fingers danced over the keys, bringing up screen after screen of information, then deleting it, Grant held his breath and stood silently behind Ray's chair.

Minutes ticked by. Each one felt like an hour to Grant. He had to get this straightened out, and soon. It had already gone too far.

When he'd joined Biddle, Hoffman and Henderson eight months ago, Grant had made up his mind that no matter how many hours or how much work it took, he'd make junior partner before his thirty-fourth birthday, then senior partner by age forty. In three months, he'd be thirty-four. His plan had been running right on schedule—before the government had thrown a monkey wrench into the works.

"Damn." He slammed his fist on the back of Ray's chair.

The clicking of the keys stopped. Over his right

shoulder, Ray sent Grant a scathing look, then went back to work.

"Sorry." Grant moved to the far side of the room and slumped into his leather desk chair. He leaned forward, rested his arms on the desktop, then riveted his gaze on the computer screen. A list of words scrolled by. Ray stopped the screen, then stared at it.

"Pay dirt!"

Jumping from the chair, Grant hurried to Ray's side. "What have you got?"

Pointing at the lower half of the screen, Ray explained. "These are the marriages of everyone named Waverly in Las Vegas in the last ten years." Slowly, the screen scrolled up. "These are all the Grant Waverlys who got married in Vegas during that time."

Grant grinned. He'd been right. There had to be fifteen or more Grant Waverlys. The government had gotten him mixed up with another Grant Waverly. Well, at least he wasn't married. He sighed. That got the biggest hurdle out of the way. One problem down and one to go.

"Hey, boss, what's your middle name? That'll help us narrow down this list some."

"Allis."

"Alice?" Ray smirked and began to chuckle.

"Allis. A-L-L-I-S. My mother's maiden name."

Staring at the screen, Ray's amusement died. "Ah...how many guys you figure would use your mother's maiden name for a middle name?"

A cold sensation chased up Grant's back. "None. Why?"

"'Cause it says here that Grant Allis Waverly married Kathleen Maureen Donovan seven years ago on April 17 at the Rose and Dove Wedding Chapel.''

Ray's words sunk in.

The stupid minister had recorded the marriage.

Almost instantly, Grant's distressed thoughts were replaced by a haunting image of him standing beneath a silk-rose-covered arch, embellished with stuffed white doves and bearing a plaque reading Love Conquers All. Beside him stood a woman. Her laughing green eyes looked up at him adoringly from a lovely face framed in unruly red curls.

Katie Donovan. His Katie.

His heart constricted with a very old, almost forgotten pain.

"KATHLEEN DONOVAN, I still say you're settling.'' Lizzie Donovan glared at her daughter over the beaded bodice of her antique wedding gown.

"For the thousandth time, Mother, I'm *not* settling for anything.''

"Pshaw! You love Chuck about as much as I love liver.''

Katie sighed. How many more times would she have to try to convince her mother that in three months, Kathleen Maureen Donovan would be marrying a man she cared deeply for? And why was she even trying?

"And I suppose being married no less than four times makes you an expert on the subject of love and marriage.'' The second the words passed her lips, Katie regretted them.

So her mother had been married four times. So she was thinking of buying the woman a wash'n'wear wedding gown for her next birthday. That wasn't Katie. She glanced at her mother. ''I'm sorry, Mother.''

''Dammit, girl, stop calling me *Mother*. Mom was always good enough until you met Chuck.''

''Charles.''

''What?''

''He prefers Charles.''

''Yeah? Well, people in hell want ice water, too, but they aren't getting it.''

''Mother!''

Her mother shook her head, then dropped the gown in a pile on the bed. She came to Katie and flung an arm around her shoulder. ''I may not know much about love, but I know plenty about divorce. And that's right where you'll be headed, if you go through with this wedding.''

Katie shuddered. That was the last word in the English language she ever wanted connected with her name. ''There will be no divorce. I'm marrying Chuck…Charles and I plan on staying married to him until I die.'' Lord, that sounded so melodramatic, even to her, but it was the truth. This marriage *would* last.

Picking up the discarded gown, Katie slipped the shoulders over a padded hanger and replaced it on the closet door hook. She smoothed out the wrinkles, then turned back to her mother.

Lizzie had sat on the edge of the bed, hands folded in her lap. She screwed the gold wedding band Katie's father had given her on and off the third finger of her right hand. She'd placed it there after Katie's father had died. It was the only ring she ever wore, even during her three other marriages.

"Mother, why don't you like Charles?"

Lizzie glanced up. Her impish blue eyes sparkled, and her snow-white, upswept curls picked up the dying rays of the afternoon sun, forming a halo around her head. Katie almost laughed. Her mother was about as far from angel material as one person could get.

"I don't dislike Chuck, dear. He's perfectly passable for someone who loves him. He's just not your soul mate."

Moving to where her mother sat, Katie sank down beside her and stilled her mother's fidgeting fingers with hers. "Soul mates are something some dreamy-eyed romantic conjured up to excuse her choice of men. In the real world, women look for other things in their mates—security, dependability, companionship. Charles is all those things." She squeezed her mother's fingers gently. "I'll be happy, Mother. I promise."

Lizzie stood, gathered her coat, kissed her daughter's cheek, then walked to the door. "I hope so, sweetheart. I truly hope so." She opened the door. "Lunch tomorrow? We can go shopping for that traveling suite you saw in the boutique on St. George Street."

Katie nodded. "At noon. I'll meet you right in front

of The King's Forge.'' She smiled. ''The weatherman has promised a nice day, and the weather has stayed quite cool so the St. Augustine tourist glut shouldn't be bad. We should have St. George Street to ourselves.''

For a moment, Lizzie stared at Katie, as if she wanted to say something, then she shook her head and pulled the door closed behind her.

After her mother had gone, Katie stared out the upstairs window of the two-story Victorian house she'd bought the first year her antique shop had shown a healthy profit. Once the taillights of her mother's car disappeared around the corner, Katie let the curtain fall back in place. She flopped full-length on her canopied bed. With her fingertip, she idly traced the intricate pattern in the white candlewick bedspread. Closing her eyes, she listened as her mother's words reverberated through her mind.

Settling. Was she?

No. She knew what she wanted and it had nothing to do with heated blood, a pounding heart or fireworks exploding every time Chuck…*Charles* touched her. She'd had all that once with Grant Waverly, the big love of her college days, and found it about as substantial as a snowbank in the Florida sun.

Charles might love his job as an economics professor, but that's all it was—a job. He left it at the college when he came home. Grant had lived, eaten and breathed his career. Making it in the world of law had mattered more to him than a life with her. If she'd married Grant, she'd be in the same place her mother had been with her father—lonely and forgotten. The fact that her mother had always kept the surname Donovan did little to change Katie's view of her mother and father's marriage. By walking out on Grant when she had, Katie had at least saved herself the trauma of a life like her mother's and eventual divorce.

Just thinking the word sent chills racing up Katie's spine. Because of her mother's track record, Katie had waited four years before accepting Charles's proposal, just to make sure that it was the real thing and that she never ended up in a divorce court. Katie would be married once and only once in her lifetime.

And if planning her future at the age of thirty with a solid, stable man was settling, then yes, she was settling. Settling for a secure life with a man who put her above his career, a man more interested in being with his family than the net earnings on his pay stub.

Despite her strong thoughts on the subject, her traitorous mind conjured up an image of Grant Waverly as she'd seen him last, standing in the parking lot of the small college she'd attended. The autumn wind had blown a wave of black hair over his brow. Her fingers had itched to smooth it back, but she'd fought the urge, afraid that one touch would melt her resolve to leave. His brown eyes had implored her to change her mind, but he never said the words that would have kept her there.

Katie rolled over on the bed and pressed a hand to her heart, amazed that the pain of that parting seven years earlier still had the power to steal her breath.

GRANT HUNG UP THE PHONE. The Las Vegas Bureau of Records had verified what he and Ray had found on the computer. He was indeed married to Katie Donovan, and had been for seven years.

"Well, boss, what are you gonna do?" Ray popped another Oreo in his mouth and swung the swivel chair to face the man slumped behind the desk.

Running his hand through his hair, Grant shook his head. "Damned if I know." A recalcitrant wave fell back to his forehead. He left it. "I guess I'll get an annulment." He stood and once more began pacing the length of his plush office. "What else can I do?"

The paralegal slid down in the chair and stretched his long legs out in front of him. "I'd think about that, boss. Didn't you say that being married was a requirement for this junior partnership thing they want to give you?"

Grant stopped pacing. Daniel Henderson's words ran through his mind. *...we like our top men to be happily married.*

"How will they know if I start annulment proceedings? I can do it quietly, then at the right moment, after I've gotten the partnership, I can say we had such differing life-styles that we decided we'd be happier single." He looked at Ray for approval.

Ray? He must be desperate if he looked to his cookie-eating paralegal for advice on how to run his life. But hell, right now he'd listen to the Three Stooges, if they could find a way out of this mess.

"Sounds okay to me, but suppose in the meantime, they want to meet Mrs. Waverly?"

"Why would they?" Then Grant remembered things like the Christmas party, where attendance by spouses was almost mandatory. Furiously, Grant scoured his mind for an answer. "I can say she's... away...doing her job."

"As what?"

Stepping over Ray's extended legs, Grant stared down at the paralegal. Dark cookie crumbs lay in a well near his waist where the T-shirt had bunched. "Dammit, Ray. I don't know. She majored in history. She could be doing anything. Maybe she chases polar bears in the Arctic. Maybe she's a roving reporter. I'll think of something. That's a minor detail." Grant went to the window of his corner office and looked out over the sun-drenched Miami skyline. "It's not like I'm breaking the law or anything. I'm just—"

The office door opened and Alfred stuck his head in. He glanced at Ray and nodded. "Raymond." Ray waved the tips of the fingers that weren't busy holding on to his next Oreo. Alfred noted the sprinkling of cookie crumbs and the paralegal's unkempt appearance, frowned, then shifted his attention to Grant.

"I forgot to mention that Harriet and I are giving a small cocktail party at the club this weekend. We want all the candidates and their wives there." He grinned. "I guess you could say we're going to look over the little ladies." When Grant opened his mouth, Alfred raised his hand. "No excuse will be acceptable. Be there *with* Mrs. Waverly. Black tie." He cast one more disapproving look at Ray, then pulled the door closed.

Cold seeped through Grant's suit pants, the only way he knew that his legs had given out, and his butt rested on the marble windowsill.

"So much for them not meeting the 'little lady.'" Ray's voice broke into Grant's frantic thoughts. "Now what, boss?" He unfolded his lanky torso from the chair. Black crumbs cascaded to the carpet.

Grant ignored both Ray and the crumbs. He remembered seeing something in the mail a few days ago. Something he'd pulled out and set aside to read later—his alumni newsletter. The editor had listed the names and addresses of those alumni who had sent them in. Maybe Katie's was among them.

He rummaged through his desk drawers, finding nothing. Hell, what were the chances of her address being in there anyway? She had been a very methodical person in college, so it seemed reasonable that she'd still be. Sending in her address would be something she'd do. He hadn't had time. Too much work.

He looked up and spotted a pile of papers on top of a small table near the wall. On top he found what he'd been searching for. On the center page, he ran his finger down the list. Nothing.

"Mind telling me what you're looking for?" Ray came to where Grant stood and peered over his shoulder.

"A newsletter from my college alumni. I'm sure Katie's address will be in one of them."

"You're going to see her?" Ray's voice sounded as if Grant had declared war on Miami.

"Yes."

"Why?" Ray stood back to allow Grant to rifle through a small filing cabinet he kept for his personal papers. "Why don't you just ask one of your girlfriends to pretend to be Mrs. Waverly?"

Grant paused in his search. Should he tell Ray that the closest thing he'd had to a real date in the past eight months was lunch with a colleague? He could visualize Ray's laughter. "No. This is too important. I need the genuine Mrs. Waverly."

Pulling out a file holding other newsletters he'd received and never found the time to read, Grant sat on the floor and began shuffling through them.

"Yes. Here it is. Kathleen Donovan, 123 Sevilla Street, St. Augustine, Florida." He zeroed in on her maiden name. A good sign. He read the date of the issue. January of this year.

Now that he'd found her address, he just hoped she hadn't done anything stupid in the past four months—like unwittingly committing bigamy.

Chapter Two

"That suit will be a perfect weight for your Caribbean honeymoon."

Katie nodded to her mother, then slipped her shoes off her aching feet beneath the cover of the restaurant table. She sighed. The perfect end to a perfect shopping trip.

She closed her eyes briefly and let the breeze from Matanzas Bay play over her hot skin. When she opened them, Lizzie had deposited her large purse in the chair between them and was accepting the plastic-covered King's Forge menu from the waitress.

Katie was glad she'd met Lizzie earlier than planned and saved lunch until now. The day she and her mother had spent together had been one of the most placid Katie could recall since she'd announced her engagement to Charles. Now that the subject had been breached again, she worded her reply with care, hoping not to disturb the tentative peace between them.

"I think so. And it's such a terrific shade of apricot. Very tropical." Katie picked up her menu and scanned down the lunch selections, hoping her mother would follow her lead and stay away from any wedding discussion.

She loosened the barrette confining her cascade of red curls at her nape. Actually, Charles had suggested she get it cut. Katie refused. Her change of appearance to match her business life-style didn't go that far. After all, when a girl had been cursed with more freckles than she needed or wanted, she didn't destroy her best attribute by chopping it off.

She'd adjusted her Victorian wardrobe to the more conservative, more staid style a successful businesswoman would wear and left her college wardrobe days behind her. The plain business suits, no-frills blouses and tailored dresses better fit her new image. Even if her mother didn't approve.

Glancing up from the menu she'd been absently studying while her thoughts veered away from lunch, she caught her mother staring at her, a grin curving her lips. She sent Lizzie a questioning look.

"You surprised me, Katie."

Her glance slipped to Lizzie's serious frown. "Oh? How?"

"I would have thought you'd have chosen a more…conservative color for your honeymoon. I know how no-frills you've become about your hair and your clothes." She cast a disapproving glance at the gray business suit Katie had chosen for the day.

Katie captured one of her curls between her thumb and forefinger and held it out. "Irish-red doesn't make choosing clothes all that easy, so when I see something that won't have a brawl with my hair color, I grab it.''

Lizzie leaned aside for the waitress to place a glass of water near her plate, then considered Katie's hair. "How do you plan on doing your hair for the big day? Something Victorian, I hope, to complement your antique gown."

"Hmm. Maybe a Gibson girl look?"

Lizzie nodded. "Perfect." She opened the menu, then contemplated the offerings with exaggerated interest. "And what about Chuck?"

"Chuck can wear his hair any way he wants."

Lizzie laughed outright. "That's not what I meant, but now you sound like my Katie."

Unable to help herself, Katie joined in, loving the return of the old camaraderie her mother and she had shared after her father died. That had vanished after her engagement to Charles. Her mother and she seemed to spar constantly about Katie's upcoming marriage and having that old closeness again was nice. However, believing it would last was foolishness. Maybe, if she reinforced how much it meant to her to have her mother's approval, Lizzie would try harder to accept Charles.

"Thanks, Mom."

Lizzie looked up from her menu, her eyes wide and deceptively innocent. "For what?"

"For not ruining our day with an argument about Charles." She grabbed her mother's hand and squeezed. "For trying to accept him."

A huff of impatience issued from Lizzie. She drew

her hand from her daughter's and blew a wisp of hair off her forehead. A stray breeze off the Matanzas Bay quickly replaced it. "What makes you keep insisting I don't accept him? I've never had any objection to Chuck. If you truly loved him, I'd accept the reincarnation of Rasputin as a son-in-law."

Ire rose in Katie like one of Florida's sudden summer thunderstorms, strong and instantly out of control. "Just what gives you the right to judge whether or not I love Charles? Need I remind you that you're about to sign divorce papers for the third time since Daddy died? Finding and recognizing love doesn't seem to be your strong point, Mother." She leaned forward and lowered her voice. "Charles loves me and he's dependable. He puts me before his career. That's what matters most to me."

For a flash second, Lizzie's eyes reflected the pain Katie's thoughtless words had inflicted.

Damn!

Would she never learn to control her cursed, quick temper? Katie had gotten so used to defending her decision to marry Charles that Lizzie had only to say his name anymore and Katie took up her battle stance, fangs bared and ready to fight.

"And what about you? I don't hear any ardent declarations of love from you. If you could tell me, with real conviction, that you love this man, I might accept this marriage."

Opening her mouth to answer her mother, Katie snapped it closed. For the first time since she'd accepted Charles's proposal, she realized she'd never told him she loved him.

BY THE TIME Katie pulled her minivan into her driveway, the sun had started to nudge the horizon. Her nerves were frayed from her recent row with her mother. Her feet hurt from walking the uneven surface of St. George Street. Her once pristine suit was rumpled. And more than one rebellious curl had escaped the confines of her barrette. In short, she was a mess. If she hurried, she'd have just enough time before Charles picked her up for dinner to repair the damage.

Katie had no idea how long it would take to repair the damage her impetuous words had done to the relationship between her mother and her.

Dammit, Mother. You know all the buttons to push to ignite my Irish temper. And once ignited, it spread through her like a flash fire, then her brain disengaged and her mouth took over.

How could she make Lizzie understand that she really cared for Charles? Even if his fastidious ways sometimes got under her skin, and she wanted to urge him to just cut loose. As usual, Katie would call her mother tomorrow after they'd both cooled off, and apologize. Lord, but she'd be glad when the wedding had faded into the past. She wasn't sure how much more her nerves could stand. One more upheaval and she'd scream.

Katie raised her gaze to the building in front of her.

As always, the sight of her home soothed her nerves and filled her with contentment and pride.

Absently, as she climbed from the car, she noted that the railing-high azaleas lining the wide, open front porch were starting to show signs of their fuchsia blossoms. Charles had been hinting that she should have them trimmed, but when she curled into the porch swing in the evening to unwind after a busy day in the shop, Katie liked the privacy the overgrown bushes afforded her. With a heavy sigh, she dragged her tired body from the van.

Not until she'd stepped to the rear of the vehicle to gather her packages did she notice the low-slung, sporty red car parked in front of her house. It reminded her of the car she and Grant had made love in the first time. However, this car probably had a heater. Grant's hadn't. If not for an old blanket and the heat their lovemaking had generated, they would have both caught pneumonia from cavorting nearly naked in the cold Connecticut winter.

Now, where had that idea come from? Shaking away the disquieting thoughts, she admonished herself.

You're thirty, Katie, not some speed-hungry, thrill-happy college junior.

Despite her stern self-admonishment, she looked back at the serviceable minivan Charles had helped her pick out and wondered what it would be like to speed down the road in the little sports car.

Nonsense thoughts. The minivan was a much more practical choice. Still, she threw one more envious glance toward the sports car, then gathering her bags, she slammed the hatchback shut. Katie climbed the front stairs to the double oak doors, shifted her burden, and inserted the key in the lock. As she turned the key, several packages slipped to the floor.

"Horse feathers!" She bent to retrieve them.

"Can I help?"

Katie jumped, snatching her key from the lock for protection. She turned on the intruder and came eye to eye with Grant Waverly for the first time in almost seven years.

Katie went numb all over. The remaining bundles joined the others on the floor. Somewhere in the back of her mind, amazement registered at her quick recognition of him. Saint Peter greeting her arrival home might have surprised her less.

Placing her hand over her fluttering heart, she cleared the sudden tightness from her throat. "Grant? Where did you come from?"

His easy smile, one she remembered all too well, oozed over her tangled nerve endings.

"Hello, Katie." Beneath her palm, her heart rate accelerated. "I've been waiting over there." He pointed to the wicker swing concealed behind the overgrown bushes. "I hope you don't mind."

"How did you find me?"

"Alumni newsletter."

His voice seemed different, deeper, but if the familiar feeling of plush velvet passing over her skin was anything to go by, it hadn't changed that much.

Katie stared at him openmouthed, struggling to

form a coherent thought. As if tempting her, that lock of black hair, the one she'd loved burying her fingers in, fell over his forehead. She curled her hands into fists. His conservative gray suit molded his muscular torso, but the bright blues and reds in his tie reminded her that under all that starch lay a man who could live and love with equal passion.

It took her a minute to realize he'd been waiting for her to say something. She shook herself mentally.

"Newsletter?" Her voice came from somewhere beyond her control. "What are you doing here?"

"We need to talk."

"Talk? After seven years?" What could they possibly have to talk about? "I don't understand."

"You will, but—" Grant looked around him "—I think we'd better go inside. I don't think you'll want your neighbors to overhear our conversation." He gathered the bags strewn at her feet.

She didn't like the ominous note in his voice at all. But even more, she didn't like the idea of him coming into her home. Why? Grant Waverly hadn't been a part of her life for seven years. He held no threat for her. Besides, short of outright rudeness, she saw no way around his request.

Scolding herself for being foolish, Katie nodded. Willing her shaky legs to move, she turned to unlock the door.

"Better let me do that. You hang on to your packages." As he handed her the bags, then removed the key from her trembling fingers, his warm flesh slid over hers.

Katie recoiled, rubbing at the spot where his hand had touched hers against her skirt. When he'd opened the door for her and stepped aside, Katie squeezed past, making sure not to touch him again. She had no idea why the tingle had spread up her arm like a forest fire in a Florida cypress grove, but she wasn't about to let it happen again. Not with Grant Waverly. Not with the man who had burned her once before and left wounds that had scarred her heart forever.

Leaving the packages on an old valet's bench in the foyer, she led him into the living room. She needed time. Time to think. Time to get accustomed to seeing him again. Time to repair her jangled nerves. "Can I get you something? Coffee? A drink?"

"Coffee would be fine." Grant watched her leave. He checked out the room. Home decor would prove infinitely safer than thinking about the way his heart had sped up when they'd touched on the porch.

The house smelled of lemon oil and musky pot-pourri and reminded him of the times Katie had dragged him through one museum after another in college. She'd always loved old things—furniture, clothes, people. The newsletter said she'd been quite successful with an antique business. That she'd wanted to spread her love of antiquated relics around didn't surprise him.

Everywhere, the house boasted the patina of years of loving care. Cypress floors, ornate oak woodwork, a Chippendale writing desk under a bay window. At the tall windows, delicate, lace curtains shifted in the breeze around potted plants, both adding just the right touch to the room. Nothing like the cold chrome and leather of his modern apartment in Miami. Everything in sight said *Katie*.

The clatter of silver and china drew his attention to the archway through which Katie had disappeared. She strode in barefoot, carrying a silver tray with a white doily beneath a gleaming silver coffee service and two bone china cups and saucers. Still couldn't keep a pair of shoes on her feet. How many times had he found her shoes in his car after a date?

As she poured their coffee, Grant eyed Katie. She'd changed since college. Filled out. In all the right places. He didn't much care for her changed taste in clothing, but it pleased him unreasonably that she'd kept her hair long, even if she did have it anchored at her neck like an old-maid aunt.

She smoothed her skirt behind her legs, then sat on the edge of the winged, fireside chair, her cup balanced perfectly on her palm. When had she become so...stiff? His Katie had been confident, but relaxed. Methodical, but spontaneous. This woman looked like she'd snap in a breeze.

"What was it you wanted to talk about?"

A large obstruction formed in Grant's throat. Telling her about their mutual problem should be simple. He'd rehearsed the words all the way from Miami. Where had they gone? Well, in for a dime, in for a dollar...or whatever that saying was his grandmother had.

"Katie, do you recall the time in college that we all went to Las Vegas for spring break?"

Her straight back became even straighter. When she glanced his way, he got a glimpse of her greener-than-green eyes. The air seemed to thicken, making breathing harder. He inhaled a large gulp of air and waited for her reply.

"Yes. I remember."

"Do you remember the minister we hired to... marry us?"

She took a sip of her coffee. He noted the slight tremble in her hand and the soft clatter of the cup trying to find its base as she sat it on the saucer.

"You mean the pretend marriage?"

"Yes."

"What about it?"

Grant took a deep breath. Suddenly, he felt as if he were about to face the toughest jury to whom he'd ever argue a case. If he fouled this up, his future at Biddle, Hoffman and Henderson could go up in smoke. Aside from all Katie's wonderful qualities, he knew her to be the typical immovable object when backed against a wall. If he wanted her to go along with his plan, then he had to break this as gently as possible. But how did a person go about telling another person gently that they were *kind of* married? It was like being *almost* pregnant.

He marshaled his stamina for the long haul and prayed.

"Well, it seems the minister misunderstood." He glanced at Katie. Her eyes had become as large as the cup she'd carefully placed back on the tray. "I'm sorry, Katie, but he recorded the marriage with the State of Nevada."

"That…" She paused, took a deep breath, then swallowed. "That means—"

"—that we're legally married," he finished for her. "Have been for seven years."

Her stricken expression and the flutter of her hands drew Grant's attention. On her left hand, a large diamond sparkled back at him. No wedding band. He breathed a sigh of relief. He attributed the emptiness that invaded him to what her engagement might mean to his plan to ensure his promotion. What else could it possibly be? He'd gotten over Katie a long time ago.

"Katie?"

She didn't answer. She just stared past him, her expression glazed.

"Katie? Are you okay?"

She nodded dumbly, stood, then walked to the desk in the bay window. For a moment, she fumbled with a stack of envelopes, as if searching for something, then she pushed them aside, shook her head and walked back to the chair. Just as she started to sit, she pitched sideways. Grant vaulted toward her, catching her moments before she hit the floor. Katie had passed out cold.

THE PLEASANT SMELL of a spicy aftershave filled Katie's nostrils. Familiar. Sexy. Masculine. Grant's aftershave.

Grant!

Her eyes flew open. Not two inches from her, Grant's face hovered, his expression filled with concern.

"You okay?"

Bolting upright, she slid to the end of the Victorian sofa. "Of course I'm all right. What makes you think I'm not?" She lifted her hair off her forehead with a shaky hand, then smoothed the added wrinkles from her skirt.

"I sort of got a hint that something might be wrong when you collapsed into my arms."

Her gaze snapped to his. That damn smile of his appeared again, the one that made her insides do aerial maneuvers. "I did no such thing."

"'Fraid so."

"Well, what can you expect? I don't get this kind of news every day." She stood and moved to the other side of the room, increasing the space between them. "Besides, it's preposterous. We can't be married. The ceremony was a lark, a..." A joke. The one thing she'd wanted so badly and never got—to become Mrs. Grant Waverly—and it had all been a joke.

"Are you saying you don't believe me?" Grant had followed her, closing the safe distance to a few feet.

Not nearly enough room for her to keep her equilibrium intact. She moved away. "That's exactly what I'm saying."

Picking up the French telephone from the writing

desk, Grant held it out to her. "Then call the marriage license department in Las Vegas."

Katie took the phone. While Grant read her the number off a piece of paper he'd pulled from his pocket, she dialed. A few minutes later, after she'd made the clerk at the other end of the line check several times, she could no longer dispute Grant's claim. They were indeed married.

Slowly, she handed the phone back to him and watched numbly as he replaced it on the desk. Oddly, her exploding world left the familiar room untouched. Her light laughter held a hysterical edge. "This can't be. I'm getting married in a little over three months."

"Not unless you want to commit bigamy."

Good grief. He was being so cool about this whole thing. Her head began to throb. She reached behind her neck and unfastened the barrette. Her hair tumbled around her shoulders, but the pain in her head stayed put.

"I've got my reception booked, my cake ordered…"

"Katie?"

"…my gown bought, my veil…"

"Katie?"

"…my honeymoon suit. I just bought my honeymoon suit." She centered her gaze on Grant.

The plea in her eyes tore at his heart. "Katie!" Grant cut through her babbling with his best courtroom voice. "All that means nothing, if you're still married to me." He didn't comment on the fact that the one thing she hadn't mentioned was that his and

Katie's unexpected marital status would keep her from marrying the man she loved. Curious.

"Then we'll have to get a d...di..." She couldn't seem to make the word pass her lips.

"Divorce?"

"Yes. No!" Katie whirled on him. "I will not have that word attached to my name." She paused. "How could you do this to me?"

"Me? As I recall, that little charade seven years ago was done by mutual consent."

"Well, undo it."

Grant's head swam. Her train of thought was harder to follow than a salmon swimming upstream. "What do you suggest?"

Her glare seared him to the bone. "You're a big-city lawyer now, aren't you?" He nodded. "Then think of something."

"I see you're just as pigheaded and unreasonable as ever. Always wanting what you can't have."

Suddenly, she stopped her frantic movements and stared at him. In the depths of her green eyes Grant read hurt. "I never asked anything more of you than a man who loved a woman should give." He had to strain to hear her whispered words.

Without warning, Grant felt the pain of their parting all those years ago burn through his gut. He couldn't go there. "We're getting off the subject. If you'll just sit down, we can discuss this rationally."

At first, he thought Katie would fight him, but she finally sat in the fireside chair. Again, she stiffened her back like a ramrod and hoisted her chin. "What do you suggest we do?"

Following her lead, Grant flopped onto the sofa where he'd laid Katie after she fainted. "It takes three months to finalize a divorce in Florida. If I file for annulment when I go back, you'll have your freedom in time for your wedding."

She looked askance at him. "You'd do that for me?"

"Katie, I don't want to be your husband any more than you want to be my wife."

She flinched, as if he'd dealt her a physical blow. "Right." On her feet again, she paced to the marble fireplace. "You're forgetting one little thing, Grant."

"What?"

"I know you. You want something."

She could still read him like yesterday's newspaper. Gathering his courage, Grant got ready to deal her the final blow, the blow that would determine his future. "I just need you to do one tiny favor for me."

She whirled on him. "I knew it. You can't just be nice for the sake of being nice, can you? There always has to be that *but*."

He leaned toward her, his hand outstretched. "Katie, this is important. It could mean the difference between me getting an important promotion and not getting it."

Pointing an accusing finger at him, she narrowed her eyes. "I should have known it had something to do with your almighty career." She laughed mirthlessly and turned away to sit in the chair she'd just vacated. "How did I ever get the idea that you came here out of common decency?"

Guilt riding heavy on his shoulders, Grant tried to explain. "I have been put on a list for a possible junior partnership. The only thing is that the senior partners had a security check done and found out about our...marriage. They're particularly partial to their junior partners being married."

Katie raised her gaze to his. Were those tears in her eyes? "And where do I fit into this picture?"

"The board is giving a cocktail party this weekend to look over the wives of all the candidates. I need you to attend the party with me...as Mrs. Waverly."

"Are you nuts?"

She gaped at him, her green eyes sparkling like hot emeralds. He'd forgotten how lovely an irate Katie could be. He breathed deeply.

"For heaven's sake. It's only one night, a few hours. Not a lifetime commitment."

"As if you'd know the meaning of that."

A stab of pain arrowed through Grant. Katie still knew how to send the zingers home with her sharp tongue.

"And after the party? What about if they want to look me over again? What happens then?" She kept her gaze trained on him. "Will you come looking for me again?"

"It won't be like that. I'll tell them you're away working on your job. After a few months, I can tell them we've decided mutually that our relationship isn't working and have agreed on an amicable divorce."

"Annulment."

"Annulment." Grant ran his finger around the collar of his shirt.

Katie looked at her hands. "Let me get this straight. I come to Miami so your senior partners can inspect me like a bug under a microscope, then you'll give me a di…an annulment."

A ray of hope blossomed in Grant. Was she going to do it? "That's right."

For a long moment, she sat quietly, then she turned to him and smiled sweetly. "No."

"No?" Leaping to his feet, Grant glared at her. His patience had reached its limit. Fury boiled inside him. "What do you mean, no?"

"Simple. N-O. No. With your brilliant lawyer's mind, you should be able to grasp the concept of *no*. I refuse to be put on exhibition just so you can get a promotion."

Okay. She wanted to play hardball. He could play just as hard as the next guy. "If you don't do this, you won't get your divorce."

"Annulment."

"Whatever. The deal is still the same. No interview, no annulment."

Katie rose from her chair, her Irish temper dripping from her eyes. "You…you… How dare you blackmail me."

Feeling more like a jerk than ever before in his life, Grant nodded. "Call it what you will. The bottom line

is this—if you want your freedom to marry…
whatever his name is—"

"Chuck…er, Charles."

"Charles. You'll come to Miami, Katie, and play
my loving, devoted wife for a few hours."

She wanted to fly at him and beat him bloody. How
dare he back her into a corner? It irked her to the
bone that she had no avenue of escape open to her.
To marry Charles, she'd have to pretend to be Grant's
wife. She saw no other choice. And to think that at
one time she loved this man beyond all reason. To
think that she'd been ready to marry him, to give him
babies, to spend her life at his side. She must have
been insane.

"All right, Grant. You win. I'll do it, but I want
you to start the papers for the annulment as soon as
you get back to Miami."

"What guarantee do I have that you'll keep your
part of the bargain?"

"My word, damn you! Unlike you, I don't make
promises I have no intention keeping." Now why had
she brought that up? The last thing she wanted was
to rehash past mistakes. He might get the erroneous
notion that she cared.

"That includes doing whatever it takes to pull this
off."

Katie's heart thumped. Her traitorous mind conjured up an instant picture of two college kids in the
back of a sports car on a cold December night.
"*Whatever it takes?* What does that mean?"

"Within reason," Grant quickly added. He pulled

a scrap of paper from his pocket. "Here. This is the address of the Miami Yacht Club. Meet me there an hour before so we can get our stories straight."

He handed her the paper. Then stepped back, as if she might take a swing at him. Prudent man.

"By the way, it's a black-tie affair. Wear something glamorous." His gaze trailed over her gray suit. "Something colorful."

"Don't push your luck, Waverly," Katie hissed.

"Kathleen?"

Both she and Grant whirled toward the voice. Charles stood in the doorway, a frown knitting his perfectly shaped brows. Katie collapsed into the chair, which magically appeared behind her.

How in heaven's name would she tell Charles that she'd just agreed to play the part of a loving wife to a man she'd been married to for seven years?

Chapter Three

"I absolutely forbid this, Kathleen!"

Charles and Katie had argued about her going to Miami for over two hours. That rat Grant had left shortly after Charles arrived at her house, leaving her to explain. For two cents, she'd call Grant and tell him what he could do with his annulment. And for two cents more, she'd tell Charles what he could do with his overbearing, chauvinistic attitude.

"Charles, I don't see that we have a choice here. Grant made it quite clear that he would not give me the annulment if I didn't show up for this damned party."

"Cursing is not ladylike, nor is it necessary."

Yes, it was. The way she felt, Katie would like to turn the air in the classy restaurant a deep, ugly purple, just on general principle. Maybe then she'd feel better about this whole mess.

"Sorry. I'm just very upset."

Patting her hand in a way Katie read as condescending, Charles glanced around them. Heaven forbid they should draw attention. He lowered his voice to just above a whisper. "Think of my position in this, Kathleen. You're asking me to allow my future wife to spend an evening pretending to be the wife of a man she was infatuated with in college."

Dammit! It wasn't an infatuation. Infatuations didn't end with your heart being lacerated. And she wasn't *asking* him anything. She was *telling* him. But she'd learned long ago that demands went right over Charles's head. If she wanted anything from him, pampering his ego was the only answer.

"Grant Waverly means nothing to me. Would I have agreed to marry you, if I still had feelings for Grant? I haven't seen the man in seven years, Charles. Even you must agree that's a bit long to hang on to a crush." She took Charles's perfectly manicured hand in hers. "I've never looked at another man since we met."

He smiled. She thought fleetingly that his smile did nothing to her insides like Grant's did. But wasn't that safe? Wasn't that the way she wanted it? This man beside her was a good man who would never let ambition cloud his love for her. And she would make him a good wife—no matter what her mother thought.

Good grief. She'd forgotten Lizzie. She'd have to break this news to her, too. Then again, why? It would all be over within a few hours and then the annulment would put an end to any connection she would ever have with Grant. Lizzie didn't have to know. Besides, Katie couldn't tolerate the thought of her mother's reaction to this.

"All right."

Charles's voice dragged Katie from her thoughts.

"I'll agree. But only because there's no other way to free you to marry me." He kissed her cheek discreetly. Before Katie could say anything, he raised his hand to stop her. "There is one stipulation. I will take you to Miami and drive you home."

"But—"

"It's either that way or not at all, Kathleen. I will not have my future wife wandering around a city like Miami without me there to protect her."

Katie relaxed. Charles could be very sweet. "Thank you." One hurdle down. Now, all she had to do was get through the party without making a colossal blunder and giving away the game.

KATIE SCOOPED UP the hem of her black evening dress and jumped a small puddle. Careening past the parking valet, she headed for the brightly lit Miami Yacht Club's front door. Thanks to the traffic, she and Grant would have about three minutes to rehearse their story.

Pushing open the door, she dropped the hem of the gown, smoothed the silky fabric, then plastered a smile on her lips.

Give 'em hell, Katie Maureen. Give 'em hell. The words her father had whispered to her on one of the few times he'd shown up for a school function and just before she'd walked onstage for her fourth-grade class play, echoed through her mind. "I'll try, Dad."

"Where in hell have you been?" Grant's whisper pulled her from her thoughts.

"Sorry. Traffic."

He grabbed her arm. Ushering her to the side of the elegant foyer, he pushed her ahead of him behind a potted palm. "We're not going to have much time. I figure the closer we stick to the truth, the easier it'll be to pull this off."

Katie barely heard him, she was too busy admiring how handsome he looked in a tux. After getting used to his signature ripped jeans and T-shirts in college, seeing him like this was a bit like taking a punch to her solar plexus. The man had absolutely no right to look so...delicious.

"Katie." He shook her arm. "Pay attention. This is no time for dreaming."

Right. No time for dreaming. Where Grant was concerned, dreaming took up precious time he could be using to plan the decor of a corner office in some big law firm. The reminder of his priorities brought Katie's floundering emotions back to earth with a jolt.

Craning her neck to see past the fauna, she looked around the foyer. "Is anyone here yet?"

"They're all here," Grant snapped. "I've spent the last hour making excuses about your absence. I told them you had to work late."

"At what?"

"Grant, what on earth are you doing hiding this charming lady behind a potted plant?"

A distinguished-looking man in a tailored tux smiled at Katie and drew her onto the open floor. Tall and slender, he carried himself well. His salt-and-pepper hairline had moved back several inches on his scalp, and his gray eyes seemed to assess her with a kind inquisitiveness.

"Hello, Alfred. May I present my wife, Katie."

He grasped her hand in a firm shake. "Alfred Biddle." He smiled and nodded approvingly at Grant.

Grant smiled down at her. Guess she'd passed through the first muster. His breath stopped dead. For the first time since he'd spotted her coming through the door, Grant really looked at Katie. His heart rate picked up a couple of hundred extra beats. He'd told her to dress glamorous and colorful, but she'd outdone herself. Black might not be colorful, but with her mane of red hair, it enhanced her beauty as no other color could have. The strapless neckline, concealed beneath a black organdy jacket, left her freckled shoulders and her swanlike neck virtually bare, making for an alluring stretch of Grant's imagination. Except for small onyx earrings, she wore no jewelry. Elegance in simplicity.

"Isn't that right, Grant?"

Grant shook himself from his sensual stupor and tried to answer Alfred. "Excuse me, sir?"

"Mind wandering, Grant?" Alfred smiled, then turned back to Katie. "This husband of yours is always thinking about work."

Katie glanced at Grant, then smiled sweetly at Alfred. "Don't I know it."

As if someone had delivered a painful pinch to his conscience, Grant flinched mentally. Putting his hand behind Katie's waist to guide her forward, Alfred moved them slowly toward the main ballroom.

"Well, tonight I'm declaring a moratorium on business. If he even thinks business, you tell me and we'll decide on a suitable punishment." He chuckled heartily at his own joke.

Inwardly, Grant groaned. It looked like a long night ahead.

Halfway into the ballroom, a white-haired woman wearing a lavender satin gown met them. Her grandmotherly face creased in a welcoming smile. "Hello, Grant." She turned to her husband. "Alfred, darling, who is this lovely woman I've caught you escorting?"

"Mrs. Biddle." Grant stepped forward, using the introductions as an excuse to rescue Katie from his boss. He slid his arm around her waist and drew her to his side. For a moment, all he could think of was how well she still fit there. Then, he shook himself back to reality. "Harriet, may I present my wife, Katie?" He turned to Katie. "Harriet is Alfred's wife."

Katie smiled and extended her hand. "Hello, Mrs. Biddle."

"Harriet, dear. Just plain Harriet. Alfred is the starched member of this family. I prefer first names." Harriet laughed and took Katie's hand. "Welcome to our little family. I'm hearing wonderful things from Alfred about your husband. Such a hard worker. Alfred has plans for him."

"Really?" The look Katie threw Grant's way said she had her own plans for Grant and none of them included an office with a view.

"Oh, yes." Harriet drew Katie from beneath Grant's arm.

Walking with her toward their table, Harriet chattered on, leaving Alfred and Grant to bring up the rear. Knowing Harriet's penchant for digging into the lives of people she'd just met, Grant worried that he wouldn't be able to run interference for Katie. He tried to catch up, but was deterred by Daniel Hoffman.

"Grant. Is that beauty you've been watching like a hawk the little woman?"

Grant cringed. He hated that term *little woman*. In his opinion, it demoted a woman to a submissive role in her husband's life as much as *the wife* did. "Yes, sir, that's Katie."

"Stunning."

He'd get no argument from Grant. The woman had heads turning all around the room, male and female. His chest expanded just a fraction. His wife. His Katie. *Only for tonight,* he warned himself. He couldn't get used to thinking of her as any more than a temporary thing. After all, Katie was engaged to another man. The thought effectively sobered him.

"I HAVE TO TELL YOU that when Alfred came home and told me the news, I was stunned, to say the least. Of all the men in the office that might keep a wife secret, Grant was the last I'd have expected." Harriet fluffed the skirt of her gown, then took the seat Alfred held out for her across the table from Katie. "How long have you two been married?"

"Seven years," Katie said, when she had a chance to slip in an answer.

"Six years." Grant's voice joined hers from over her shoulder.

Harriet blinked. "Well, which is it?"

Glaring at Grant, Katie turned an apologetic smile to Harriet. "It's seven. You know men. They can never keep track of things like that."

Harriet laughed. "I know just what you mean. My Alfred told everyone for the longest time that my birthday was July fifteenth when it's the seventh of January. His excuse was that both months began with a *J*. He considered that close enough."

Grant had taken a seat next to Katie. She leaned over and whispered in his ear. "Where did six years come from? Don't go changing the rules on me midstream. You said to stick as close to the real facts as we could."

Grant caught Harriet observing them from across the table. He smiled. "I thought it sounded more realistic," he said in a whisper.

"Well, stop thinking. You're confusing me."

He glanced at Harriet and Alfred, then chucked Katie under the chin. "Yes, dear."

Lout. Treat her like some three-year-old, would he? She'd teach him. Leaning toward him, she smiled sweetly, then kissed his ear. His eyes widened and his face grew red. *Bingo!* She smirked at him, then turned back to the group gathering at their table.

Put that in your pipe and smoke it, Grant Waverly.

Katie did a mental search for a safe subject, preferably one that did not entail her knowing too much about a relationship that didn't exist. "Harriet, I just love your gown. Such a lovely shade of lavender. Very becoming."

"Why, thank you. I got it in... Dear me, what is the name of that shop in West Palm?" She looked at Katie. "You must know the one I mean, green-and-white awnings. Very pricey."

Katie shook her head. "I don't get down that way often."

"*Up*," Grant interjected. "She doesn't get *up* that way." He wrapped her shoulders in a bear hug and kissed the tip of her nose. Katie's blood pressure shot to the top of the scale. "My poor Katie has a lousy sense of direction." He tweaked her nose. "Isn't that right, sweetheart?"

Tweaked! He tweaked her nose! Under the table, Katie stomped down on his instep with her three-inch heel. He flinched, but she had to admit, covered his pain quite well. She felt his hand slip her purse off her lap and onto the floor.

"Oh, sorry, darling. I knocked your purse off. Let me help you find it." He grabbed her arm and dragged her under the white tablecloth with him.

"What are you doing?" Katie pulled her arm away.

"What am *I* doing? For one thing I'm trying to convince these people that we're in love, not crippling you. Do that again, Katie Donovan, and I'll—"

"You'll what? Squeal on me?" She smiled. "I don't think so."

"Need help?"

Katie glanced up to see Alfred's florid face peering at them from beneath the other side of the tablecloth. "No. Thanks." She held up the purse. "Got it."

Once more erect, Katie avoided the glances of the other diners at the table. Damn Grant Waverly. What ever possessed her to agree to this nightmare comedy?

You want an annulment, her conscience reminded her. *You want to be free of this man beside you once and for all.*

With the reminder, she settled back into her role of the loving wife, but despite the bright lights, the glittering jewels and the sparkling evening clothes, the room seemed to have dimmed.

GRANT'S GAZE followed Katie around the dance floor. He never should have let her dance with Alfred. God only knew what the crazy woman was saying. Besides, he didn't much like how close Alfred was holding her. He checked his watch. Just another hour or so and they could make a discreet getaway and this eternal evening would be behind him and his promotion would be in front of him.

Thoughts of his promotion brought a smile.

"My, but it's evident you love her." Harriet's voice cut into his thoughts. "You haven't taken your eyes off her since she started dancing with my Alfred." She leaned closer. "I can assure you, Grant, he's quite harmless, if you know what I mean." She sent him a wink.

Patting himself on the back mentally for pulling this off, Grant dragged his gaze from the dance floor.

Actually, if he wanted to be fair, Katie had pulled it off more than he had. She'd been gracious and congenial. Her natural charm had won over everyone at their table.

"So, Grant," Harriet continued, "you were saying Katie worked tonight, but you didn't say what she does."

Frantically, Grant searched his mind. If he planned on using incompatible life-styles as the reason they divorced later, he had to give Katie an occupation more threatening than an antique dealer.

"She's a photographer for one of those nature magazines." Not a doubt existed in his mind that Katie would kill him for this lie. Katie didn't have a technical bone in her body, and as far as cameras were concerned, she'd never perfected the art of getting her subject's entire body in the photo. But then, after tonight, no one at the firm would ever see Katie again.

"She travels to all those out-of-the-way places and photographs native tribesmen and their life-style. She's gone a lot. Makes life very difficult, sometimes. I really miss her." That should very nicely lay the groundwork for the upcoming divorce.

"Really? How interesting." Harriet pointed toward the dance floor. "Here they come. I can't wait to ask her about her work. It sounds very adventuresome."

Before Grant could stop Harriet, Katie and Alfred arrived back at the table. Grant held Katie's chair. Her hair brushed over his hand as he pushed the chair under her. The sensation brought back a cascade of memories. Unable to stop himself, he caressed a curl before slipping back into his chair beside Katie.

Katie felt the slight tug on her scalp and knew what had happened. Grant had always been fascinated with her hair. But that he did it now, when no one could see him, surprised her. At one time, it had held special meaning for them. One of those meaningless little lovers' gestures he'd used when he wanted to say something to her without using words. Glancing at him, she saw something in his eyes that totally unnerved her, the same regret she'd seen that last day when she'd walked away.

Quickly, she tore her gaze from his and searched for a safe subject.

"Your husband is quite the Fred Astaire, Harriet. I'm sure, what with all those fancy steps he was doing, that he regretted asking me to dance." Katie bestowed a charming smile on Alfred, then slipped her shoes off beneath the table to rub her abused toes. "I'm afraid I'm not a very good dancer."

"Well," Harriet said, "that's not surprising. I'm sure you get little opportunity to dance out there with those pygmies and wild beasts."

"Excuse me?" Katie looked at Grant. He had become totally engrossed in pleating his napkin.

"On your job. Grant was telling me all about it while you and Alfred tripped the light fantastic." She looked around her, as if she were about to impart a state secret. "Tell me, do they really shoot each other with poison darts?"

"Darts?" Katie tried to catch Grant's eye for help,

but he continued to fool with his damn napkin. "I'm afraid you lost me, Harriet."

"You know. Those natives that you photograph for the magazines. Do they use poison darts?"

That did it. She couldn't stand one more minute of this game. Her head hurt. Her feet throbbed. And if Grant touched her one more time, she'd...she'd... she'd kill him. No. She'd maim him first, then she'd kill him. Either way, Grant Waverly was dead meat and she was out of here.

"Yes, they do." She stood. "If you'll excuse me, I have to repair my makeup."

Katie hurried across the dance floor and into the foyer, where she'd seen a bank of phones on her way in. Grabbing the first receiver, she dialed the hotel where she and Charles were staying.

"Hello."

"Charles. Can you come and get me?"

"The party's over?"

"It is for me."

"I'll be right there."

She hung up, then stood back, making herself as inconspicuous as possible, while making sure she could see out the front door. "Stick to the facts," she mumbled into her purse while she searched for aspirin. "Poison darts and natives. What's wrong with being an antique dealer?" No, Grant couldn't be satisfied with something so mundane, he had to make her into the female version of Ansel Adams.

Heaven help her, what had she done to deserve this evening? She glanced out the door impatiently. When

Charles got there she was going to give him a big
kiss. She really didn't appreciate that man enough.

GRANT CHECKED HIS WATCH. Twenty minutes. What
could she be doing in the ladies' room all this time?
He glanced toward the direction she'd gone.

"I'm going to do a few repairs myself, Grant. I'll
see what's keeping Katie." Harriet patted his shoulder, then disappeared across the dance floor.

If he knew Katie, she was taking her time and planning a retaliatory act against him for the photographer
thing. Who knew Harriet was interested in natives and
dart guns?

He grinned to himself. He'd forgotten until tonight
how much spicier life was with Katie in it. Having
Katie around was like going from the shade to the
sunshine. Despite everything, Grant had to admit,
he'd missed Katie. But he hadn't known how much
until she'd stomped on his instep.

HARRIET SAUNTERED into the foyer. A movement outside the doors caught her attention. A couple kissed
beside a waiting car.

Oh, my word. Katie and a strange man.

Could she be mistaken? She moved closer and
peered round the potted palm beside the front door.
No. No mistaking that mane of red curls and that
slinky black dress. It was Katie all right, and the man
wasn't Grant.

Harriet hurried to the edge of the dance floor and

frantically signaled for Alfred to join her. A few minutes later, he stood in front of her.

"Harriet, what is it?"

"Katie."

"What about her? Did you find her?"

"Oh, yes. Indeed I did."

"Well, what's the problem then?"

Grabbing her husband's jacket sleeve, she dragged him out of the flow of traffic. Looking around her to make sure no one could overhear, she cupped her hand around her mouth. "I just saw Katie kissing a strange man outside, then she got into a car with him and drove off."

Alfred rolled his eyes heavenward, then threw a peek over his shoulder in the direction Harriet's shaking finger had pointed. "You must be mistaken."

Shaking her head, Harriet stepped closer. "No mistake. Red hair. Black evening gown. No jewelry." She placed her hand over her mouth. "Oh, Alfred, what are we going to do?"

"Do?" Alfred began to pace the narrow confines of the hall she'd dragged him into. His shoes made no sound as he made several circles on the Oriental carpet. "Why do we have to do anything?"

"But, Alfred—"

"Harriet, I trusted that boy. He's my favored pick for junior partner. If he has a wife who plays around, I'll have to remove him from the list. I hate to do it, but there're other considerations—security, a government contract, the reputation of Biddle, Hoffman and Henderson."

Harriet yanked him to a halt. Alfred had spent their entire married life putting the firm first. She'd stood for it, understanding how much it meant to him, seeing as how his grandfather had helped start it. But this time, she had to put her foot down.

"To hell with the firm. The firm will survive without Grant and, as much as you may disagree with this, without you, too. I'm talking about two flesh-and-blood people. What about them? They're very much in love. It's evident in the way they look at each other. We have to do something to help *them.*"

Alfred removed his sleeve from her grasp, then smoothed the material. "What do you suggest?"

Thinking for minute, Harriet sat down on the settee provided for Yacht Club patrons. Glancing up, she looked straight at a framed painting of a sailboat making its way to a small island. Of course. Commandeering Alfred's sleeve again, she drew him down beside her.

"Blast, woman, stop pulling me around like a yo-yo." Alfred smoothed the material of his tux again.

"Forget about your grooming and listen to me. It's quite evident that aside from loving each other, Katie and Grant have marital problems. After all, they both seemed very much on edge tonight, like they were walking on eggs. What they need is time alone to heal their marriage." She pointed at the painting. "We can take them to our island in Maine. With no transportation to the mainland, no TV, what else can they do, but entertain each other...doing what comes naturally?" She winked broadly at her gaping husband.

"What if they won't go?"

She patted his hand. "Alfred dear, you're the boss. *Order* them to go." Seeing his reluctance in his expression, she waved her hand at him, dismissing the idea. "Oh, never mind. I'll take care of it. Just have Grant in your office Monday morning."

Speaking from experience, Alfred didn't doubt his wife's abilities to get her way and was secretly relieved that she'd taken the chore out of his hands. Harriet could outtalk, outmaneuver, out...she could just plain snowball anyone into doing what she wanted, and never break stride doing it.

The truth of the matter was that Grant and Katie going to Maine had become a foregone conclusion in Harriet's mind as soon as she'd decided upon her course of action, and there was little any man, woman or child could do would change it.

Chapter Four

"Maine?" Wide-eyed, Grant's gaze shifted from Alfred to Harriet.

After the fiasco the previous evening at the Yacht Club, then being summoned into Alfred's office first thing this morning, Grant expected to be called on the carpet for Katie's disappearance. To his surprise, however, Alfred and Harriet had accepted with total understanding his explanation that Katie had been taken ill and left early, then had all but ordered him to take a two-week vacation at the Biddle's Maine island home.

"Alfred and I want to get to know the candidates better. We felt that a couple of weeks on our private island would be just the thing." Harriet patted her perfectly coifed hair, then leveled a matronly smile at Grant. "Your tie is crooked, dear...do straighten it."

"Island?" As he looked to his boss for help, Grant did as he was told. "I—"

Alfred shrugged his shoulders and shifted uncomfortably in his chair. Grant couldn't recall ever seeing his staid, well-adjusted boss squirm before. Alfred threw a glance at his wife, then ran a finger around the neck of his shirt.

"You and Katie will love the island," Harriet continued, as though Alfred had faded into the fancy mahogany woodwork. "This time of year it's so beautiful...wildflowers, blue ocean, private—just the place to relax and get to know one another." Harriet's smile bordered on mawkish.

Grant knew he was missing something here, but for the life of him, he couldn't figure out what it was. Then her words sunk in. "Katie? You want Katie to come, too? But—"

"Why of course, dear." Harriet laughed. "How else will we get to know her unless she's with you? I'm sure you could tell us about her, but that wouldn't be quite the same, now would it...of course it wouldn't. You *do* want us to get to know her, don't you? I knew you would...she's such a lovely thing. You must be so proud of her and her photo accomplishments. Do uncross your legs, Grant...you'll put terrible creases in those charming trousers."

Dumbfounded, Grant grappled with an excuse as to why they couldn't accept the Biddles' invitation. But by the time he'd uncrossed his legs, smoothed his trousers and opened his mouth, Harriet had already barged on.

"We'll leave it up to you to extend our invitation to your lovely wife...I just know she'll be thrilled...who could pass up a vacation in Maine...I could, of course, issue the invitation myself...and good manners says I should...but I'm sure you'd like to break the news to her yourself...which is only right...I wouldn't spoil the surprise for anything.''

Quickly coming to realize that trying to interrupt Harriet's unending flow of words compared to stopping Hurricane Andrew, he waited for her next breath to interject an objection. Obviously, however, the woman didn't need air to survive as the rest of them did.

"We won't take no for an answer. Will we Alfred? No is just not an acceptable answer...but then, I'm certain we won't have to worry about that. Will we, Alfred?''

Frowning, Alfred opened his mouth, but before he could say anything, Harriet silenced him with a quelling glance. Neatly, she inserted herself between the two men. Harriet forged on, never missing a beat. "Now, we had planned to leave day after tomorrow...can you and Katie can be ready by then? Of course you can...I mean, it's not as if you have to pack much in the way of clothes, now is it?'' She snickered at her own foolishness. "That's not to say we wander around the island sans clothing.'' She made a tsking sound. "That would never do. Never, never.''

Day after tomorrow.

Grant came to attention in the chair. He tightened the knot of his red-and-gray silk tie, then, when spots of light began dancing before his eyes, he immediately loosened it. "I—"

"Wonderful...you made your tie crooked again, dear. Do stop fussing with it. Two days works out perfectly...Elmer, our caretaker, can open the house and bring in provisions...Elmer does get a might irritated with us non-Mainers if we arrive and don't give him proper notice...takes time away from his lobster pots, you know.'' She threw a smile over her shoulder at Alfred. "Can't have that. Isn't that right, dear?''

Like Grant, Alfred seemed to have given up on trying to add to the one-sided conversation, such as it was. Instead, he just nodded, reminding Grant of the little dolls that ducked and bobbed dumbly in the rear windows of cars.

Harriet moved a picture on the side wall a fraction of an inch, all the while still speaking. "It's all settled then. Grant and Katie will join us on the island...you won't be sorry you decided to go...there's nothing like a short vacation to keep a marriage on track. Don't you agree, Grant? Of course you do...how foolish of me to even ask.''

Helplessly watching his last avenue of escape close before his eyes, Grant smiled wanly and did his own imitation of the dumb dolls.

"You two lovebirds will come back from the island feeling like newlyweds,'' she added, picking up her purse from Alfred's desk, then heading for the door. "You *will* enjoy this,'' she chirped as the door closed behind her. Despite her cheery tone, Grant decided that Harriet's parting salvo constituted an order and not an observation.

Exhausted mentally, Grant stared at the closed door, feeling as if he'd just survived a tornado.

When he could once more think rationally and with some kind of order, he considered Katie and her reaction to all this. He hoped she'd laugh and take this as lightly as Harriet. Knowing Katie and her volatile temper, he doubted that, but hoping for it would help keep him sane. How to tell her eluded him, but one thing he knew for sure—when he did tell her, Katie would kill him.

Still, he derived a certain amount of pleasure out of paying Katie back for walking out on him last night. Making explanations had been no easy task. But, when he reminded himself of another fact, his pleasure enjoyed a short life.

He would be spending two weeks with Katie in a closed, intimate setting. After last night, could he maintain a relationship with her for two weeks and keep his male hormones under control? If nothing else, their little act had reminded him that Katie Donovan posed a danger to him he hadn't experienced since college—except now she belonged to another man.

SWIVELING HIS DESK CHAIR toward his large office window overlooking the Atlantic Ocean, Grant listened to the endless ringing of Katie's phone. After the tenth ring, he replaced the receiver in the cradle and ran his hand through his tousled hair.

How would he tell her about this new turn of events, especially after he'd promised her that the cocktail party would be the end of it? His first conclusion still held. She'd kill him. The only upside he could find to this was that, when angered, Katie was an astoundingly beautiful woman.

For a moment, he forgot about Maine and let his mind wander to how lovely she'd looked last night and how good it had felt to once more have her at his side. Just the prospect of seeing her again had the power to elevate his blood pressure several notches.

Shaking away such crazy thoughts, he picked up the receiver, punched the redial and waited while the call connected. The incessant ringing began again.

Why in hell didn't the woman at least have an answering machine? He drummed his fingers on the desktop. On the fourth ring, his office door burst open.

"What are you doing here?" Ray stood just inside the door, tapping the face of his Tweety Bird watch.

Grant cupped the receiver's mouthpiece with his hand. "I work here, remember?"

Ray strode toward the desk. "Not today you don't. You should have been in court ten minutes ago."

Grant glanced impatiently at his desk clock, hung up the phone, then grabbed for the briefcase Ray held out to him. "Damn! I forgot all about court."

"Well, you better hope Judge Johnson forgot, too. You know what a drag he is about time."

Grant needed no reminders about Johnson. The last time Grant had been late in Johnson's courtroom, the old judge had chewed on his hide for over fifteen minutes. When Grant tried to explain, Johnson had thrown in a warning for contempt of court. He started toward the door.

Katie!

He pivoted back to Ray. "You have to make a phone call for me."

"Why me?" Ray dug into his pocket for the inevitable Oreo, picked off some lint, then popped it into his mouth.

"Because you're the only one who knows what's going on with Katie." Grant spun the nob on his Rolodex. "Here, call this number until you get an answer," he added, poking a fingertip at one of the cards. "It's Katie's. Tell her Harriet Biddle has invited us to spend two weeks in Maine with her and Alfred and that I need to talk to her."

Ray swallowed and shook his head. Backing away, he held up his hand. "Not me."

Anger rising, Grant advanced on his paralegal. "Ray, you have to do this for me. I've got to get to court."

Continuing to shake his head, Ray kept his distance. "You're not siccing this Katie person on me. I don't mind helping out with your personal life from time to time, but not when it means possible bodily injury. This is something you need to take care of yourself, Counselor."

"How's she going to hurt you through the phone?"

Ray stood his ground. "I have delicate eardrums. An old college football injury."

Grant glanced at his watch again. Sighing, he conceded that Ray was right. This was his problem, not Ray's. He consulted his desk calendar and did a quick rundown of his schedule.

Today's court appearance would probably go until six o'clock. Judge Johnson was well-known for keeping everyone in the courtroom until everything was settled to his satisfaction, especially when setting out to teach a tardy counsel a lesson in courtroom etiquette. Then he had a business dinner with a client at seven. Another court appearance the next day would eat up the morning. He couldn't see getting away until noon tomorrow.

How would he be able to talk Katie into going to Maine in a day and a half? Something told him a year wouldn't be long enough. Then he remembered the annulment.

"Ray, did we file those annulment papers I gave you yesterday?"

Ray licked cookie crumbs from his fingers. "No."

Grant smiled. "Don't. There's a case of Oreos in it, if you hang on to them until Monday." By then he and Katie would be basking in the sun on a private island in Maine.

Raising one disapproving eyebrow, Ray smiled. "Dirty pool, Counselor."

Grimacing, Grant avoided his paralegal's censorious expression. "Desperate people do desperate things."

Though he sounded cavalier, guilt was digging inroads into his conscience. He felt like the worst kind of heel having to blackmail Katie into this. But, if he wanted this promotion, did he have a choice? And what about that warm glow he got every time he thought about having Katie to himself for two weeks?

"I won't use the annulment unless she backs me into a corner."

Problem was, he fully expected she'd do just that.

"...AND IF IT RAINS, we can just move the reception inside. Does that meet with your approval?" Charles turned to face Katie. "Kathleen?"

"What?" Katie gathered her wandering thoughts. They'd spent most of the morning visiting possible places to hold their reception and were discussing the details in her dining room over coffee. Unfortunately, Katie had heard very little of what Charles had been saying. "I'm sorry. I was distracted."

Distracted? A mild term for what she'd been doing. Two whole days had passed, and she continued to be preoccupied with Grant Waverly, keeping him exactly where she didn't want him and from where she had spent two days and nights trying to bar him—the forefront of her thoughts. Concentrating on wedding arrangements had become a near impossibility.

"I'm trying to get your okay on the site for the reception," Charles explained, his voice clearly showing his impatience. "Darling, you have to make a decision soon. If we wait much longer, all the good places will be booked. Most of the dates are already taken. We were lucky to find this one on the same day as our wedding."

Giving herself a mental shake, Katie pushed aside images of Grant Waverly suspended by his thumbs from a torture rack and tried to concentrate on what

Charles was saying. "I'm sorry. The church sounds fine, Charles. Call them and reserve the day."

Sighing, Charles gathered the papers, shoved them in his briefcase, then stood. "I can see you're not really into this, and I have a class in twenty minutes. We'll finish discussing this tonight over dinner." He studied her for a moment. "Kathleen, is there something bothering you? You've been strangely inattentive ever since we came back from Miami."

Forcing a smile, she hooked her arm in his and steered him toward the front door. "I'm fine, just wool-gathering."

Charles seemed to accept her explanation, which for some odd reason irritated her. Where was his assertiveness when she needed it? Why wasn't he more concerned?

But then, why should he be? He had no idea that she'd been up two nights fighting off memories of a silly college romance. He had no idea that, if she inhaled, Grant's aftershave bombarded her senses, or that, if she closed her eyes tight, she could still feel his fingers grazing her tender skin as he pushed her hair aside.

She sighed and promised herself to stop this foolishness. She'd put the whole incident behind her. It was over. She'd done her part and she'd never have to see Grant Waverly again. She had no doubt that in three months, the annulment papers would arrive, she'd sign them and that would be that. A clean break with no regrets.

At the door, Charles turned to her and took her

shoulders. "Maybe I should cancel my class and take you out for lunch. Get your mind off weddings and everything else."

"No. I'll be fine, really." She stood on tiptoe and kissed him quickly. "I think I'll just lie down for an hour and regroup. These past few days were a bit more than I'd expected. Maybe I'll go over to the store for a while this afternoon. I have a shipment of antiques coming in and pricing them should clear away the cobwebs. I've shoved enough work off on my assistant lately. It's time I helped carry the load, too."

Patting her hand, he kissed her cheek, then smiled down at her. "Very well. I'll see you tonight."

Katie closed the door behind him, then leaned her forehead against the cool glass in the sidelight. Sometimes, Charles made her feel as if she'd just kissed her brother. It would have really helped her state of mind right now if he had planted a healthy lip-lock on her to remind her who she was and what her priorities were. Unfortunately, Charles rarely did lip-lock.

And when he did, it wasn't the toe-curling experience of being kissed by Grant that she remembered from college. She cut that line of thought short. Until Grant had reentered her life, she'd been perfectly content with Charles. Now, she was doing kiss comparisons. What next?

Get your act together, Donovan!

As she returned to the dining room to gather the cups from the table, a knock sounded on her back door. Frowning, she hurried into the kitchen, placed the dirty dishes in the sink, then opened the door. A gasp of surprise issued from her. An uncharacteristically rumpled Grant stood on the threshold.

He looked like he'd been mugged.

"What happened to you?"

"Nothing. It's been a long day. Is he gone?" When she nodded, he pushed past her into the room. "We have to talk."

Closing the door, Katie placed her hands on her hips and faced him. His words brought back uncomfortable memories of the last time he'd shown up out of nowhere. "The last time you said that I ended up playing pat-a-cake with people I don't know, telling lies and pretending to be something I'm not." She walked past him and began rinsing the cups and saucers. "Thank God that's over with."

Silence followed more silence. Not just silence, but a hushed stillness that put her whole body on alert, raised the fine hairs on the nape of her neck, and had an alarm bell ringing in her head.

Slowly, she turned toward him. "It *is* over with... isn't it?"

His lopsided, half grin reminded her of a teenager whose mother had just found his supply of girlie magazines under his mattress. Beyond that, something in his expression told her her worst nightmare had not ended, but had merely taken a breather and was about to reinstate itself in an even more horrific way.

She backed away, water dripping from her hands onto the spotless green-and-white tile floor. "Oh, no.

Not again. You said that would be all you'd ever want from me.''

"I know."

"You promised."

"I know, but—"

"No buts, Grant. You promised."

"Katie—"

"Don't Katie me. Just tell me what I'm thinking is not true.''

Grant moved toward her. He extended his hands in supplication. "I wish I could."

She moved back, convincing herself that putting distance between them would ward off what he was about to say. Her back slammed into the refrigerator. Her gaze remained glued to Grant's.

Where did he begin? He decided to jump right into the middle and hope for the best. "Katie, the Biddles have a summer place on a private island in Maine and for some reason, known only to them and the gods of misfortune, they want us to join them up there for a while."

"A little while?"

"Just two weeks."

Katie's mouth fell open. "Two weeks? I hardly call two weeks a *little* while, Grant."

"Well, it's not all *that* long."

"Not that long?" She squeezed past him on her way to the sink. Leaning her hands on the edge, she looked out the window. He could see by the way her jaw worked, she was trying to contain herself. "I have a business to think of. Responsibilities. I just can't go running off for two weeks." She waved her hand. "It's academic anyway. I'm not going."

He moved next to her. "You *have* to go. This wasn't left open to argument."

She put the table between them. Her perfume lingered in the air. He took a step back from the aroma to regain his floundering composure. "Harriet wouldn't take no for an answer."

Katie laughed. "As I recall, conversing with Harriet is like trying to interrupt machine-gun fire."

"Exactly. I tried. I really did, but she wouldn't listen. Won't you reconsider?" Grant forged ahead. "You can understand what I was up against." He did not want to have to use his ace in the hole—the annulment. It would be so much easier if she just went along with him.

Katie swung on him, her green eyes shooting fire. "No! I can't understand what you were up against. You could have told them the truth, that we were married by a fluke and that we're in the process of getting an annulment and that we want to spend time with each other about as much as a mouse wants to be locked in a small closet with a hungry cat." She took a deep breath, then sunk into one of the Windsor kitchen chairs.

Slipping into the chair across from her, he folded his hands on the tabletop and stared at her profile. "Does this mean you won't go?"

Her head jerked up. Her eyes had lost none of the green fire. "What part of this don't you understand? That's exactly what it means. If you want this damned job so bad, then you figure out how to get it on your own." She hit the table with her palm. "Just give me my annulment and get out of my life."

"Uh…about the annulment."

She directed her gaze at him again. This time, he could fairly feel her anger singeing his cheeks. "You didn't file the papers, did you?"

"They'll be filed on Monday." He hoped that would appease her and take some of the sting out of what he had to do.

"Monday? What happened to two days ago? You said you'd do it as soon as you got back."

"I was busy."

"Busy? Busy doing what? Busy worrying about Grant and his career? Busy being Mr. Big-Shot City Lawyer?" She took a deep breath and threw her loosened mane of russet curls over her shoulder, obviously trying to regain her calm. "When are you going to think of someone besides yourself and what you want?"

"I told you how much this job means to me. I've worked a long time, given up a lot to get where I am. You have no idea how much I've sacrificed."

"Oh, yes, I know. I know better than anyone else. I know that love wasn't enough, that family and kids couldn't fill that void, that a loving wife didn't have a chance of competing with a place in a prestigious law firm." Katie stopped short. She stared at him wide-eyed for a moment, as though regretting her outburst, then turned away. "Go away, Grant. Go back to Miami and leave me alone."

Heart hurting for what he was about to do, Grant stood, walked to the door and placed his hand on the knob. Keeping his back to her, he uttered the words that would sentence them both to two weeks of misery, and probably have Katie hating him forever.

"I don't want to have to do this, Katie, but you forced my hand."

"Then why do it?"

"Mainly because we have to be honest with each other. In that respect, we're all we have." He took a deep breath. "I'll pick you up tomorrow night a five o'clock. Be ready, Katie, or you won't be getting married in three months, because you'll already be married." He wasn't sure if his words hurt Katie or him more.

HAVING SPENT the past hour filling her mother in on the events of the past two days, Katie dropped into the fireside chair and waited for the cross-examination she knew would follow.

Lizzie studied her daughter across the Victorian living room. "This Grant person, is he the one you wrote home about from college?"

"Yes, Mother. One and the same."

"I seem to recall that you fancied yourself very much in love with him at the time." Lizzie crossed her legs, smoothed her skirt over her knees and then balanced her cup and saucer on the palm of her hand.

Pushing her mother's words aside with a wave of her hand, Katie avoided direct eye contact. "A crush. Nothing more. I was over Grant years ago."

"Then tell me why you're going to such lengths to make his life easier? You could just tell everyone the truth and be done with it. You can end this marriage without Grant."

"I could. I could also take the chance that Grant won't agree to the annulment I need to marry Charles. I'm not up to a court battle, nor do I have the time. In three months I *have* to be a free woman."

"Really, dear? Would he be that vindictive?" Lizzie sent her a skeptical look.

An undignified huff escaped from Katie. "You don't know Grant like I do. He'd do anything to further his career. That's all he's ever cared about. His career and his advancement is what this whole mess is about."

For a long moment, Lizzie remained quiet. "Have you told Charles?"

"Yes. Last night over dinner."

"And…?"

"What do you mean *and?* Do I have to spell it out for you? His fiancée is going off to a remote island with another man for two weeks to pretend to be his wife. What would you expect from him?" She sighed. "By the time he left, he was seething. I'm not even sure he still wants to marry me." With her fingernail, Katie traced the needlepoint flower in the throw pillow. "And I can't say as how I blame him."

"If you don't mind my saying so, you don't look like a woman who may have just lost the man she loves."

"Mother, don't start on that again. I have enough

problems without having to dodge your barbs about my relationship with Charles.'' Katie took a deep breath. "I didn't have to tell you any of this."

"No, you didn't. But I'm glad you did, because it gives me the opportunity to once more point out what I've been saying all along—Charles is not for you. Maybe this two-week hiatus will give you the perspective you need to see that."

"Mother, please." Katie's voice sounded tired, even to her. How she wished it were next month, next year, anytime, but here and now.

Lizzie moved to the tray holding the coffeepot and refilled her cup. For the first time in months, Katie really looked at her mother. Lines of tension had taken up residence around Lizzie's mouth. This third divorce was taking its toll on her.

Just one more reason to add to Katie's list of why one should be sure before stepping into marriage. However, as angry as her mother made her and as much as she disapproved of her mother's personal life, Katie loved her and worried about her.

"Mother, are you okay?"

Glancing up from her cup, Lizzie fostered a weak smile for her daughter. "Sure. I'm fine. It's just that James is making this divorce more difficult than need be."

"Oh?" Katie hadn't discussed the divorce from Lizzie's fourth husband with her. She'd taken the ostrich approach and ignored it, hoping it would be over quickly.

"He wants a part of the house." Shaking her head

of snowy curls, Lizzie placed a small finger sandwich on the edge of her saucer, then returned to her seat on the couch. One recalcitrant wave fell across her forehead and with a huff of air, she sent it back to join the rest. "Of course, that's out of the question."

Katie felt her ire rise. The old ten-room Victorian house on the next block had been the only home Katie had known until she moved into her present house. Her father had built it as a wedding present for her mother, and Lizzie flatly refused to give it up, even after Katie's father's death eight years ago. Katie secretly agreed with Lizzie's decision.

Katie had always believed that her mother felt close to her father there. Lizzie had never, by word or deed, confirmed or denied this belief, but Katie went on believing it.

Despite her father's frequent absences from their lives, her parents had had a good marriage filled with love. As illogical as it sounded, after living life with a man whose job kept him on the road for most of their married life, Katie had finally decided that Lizzie couldn't live alone. She needed a man, and sex had nothing to do with it. Unfortunately, her choices in men had left a lot to be desired, as attested to by three divorces in as many years.

"I hope your lawyer is fighting the division of the house."

Taking a bite of the finger sandwich, Lizzie chewed, then swallowed. "Tooth and nail. The house is mine and will remain so until I die and it goes to you. What you do with it then is your business."

Lowering the cup to her lap, Lizzie gazed at her daughter. "I know you're sick of hearing me preach, but allow me this one last statement. Marrying the wrong person for the wrong reasons can be as painful as losing the one you truly love."

For once Lizzie's admonition about her marrying Charles didn't bring Katie's temper to a boil. What it did do astonished Katie into silence.

A vivid picture crossed her mind of a man standing in a college parking lot, calmly watching her walk away, while she closed out the sound of her heart shattering into a million pieces around her.

Chapter Five

A low, deep moan penetrated the heavy mist lying on the ocean's glassy surface, as if some great, sea beast suffered in excruciating pain.

Katie shivered. "What was that?"

"Just the foghorn at Seal Point Lighthouse." Harriet Biddle's seeming lack of concern did nothing to ease Katie's jumpiness.

She thought she had her frazzled nerves under wraps until Grant, the Biddles and she had boarded the Biddle's forty-two-foot cruiser and headed straight into this thickening wall of pea-soup Maine fog. Katie didn't do boats or water that was several hundred feet over her head, and she was quickly discovering that she didn't do fog, either. She'd never realized how much stock she put into knowing exactly where she was going and being able to see the horizon as she did so.

One other discovery she'd made was that she genuinely liked Harriet. Everything about Alfred's wife had changed. Instead of her pricey Palm Beach clothes, she wore a plain denim skirt and white camp blouse. Her hair had been tousled by the slight breeze they'd encountered at the airport and her speech had slowed to conversation speed. Her whole demeanor had become relaxed and open.

Taking her cue from Harriet, Katie tried not to think about the damp fog surrounding them. Resolutely, as the boat plowed through the battleship-gray water, she closed her eyes and allowed the soothing effect of the waves to seep into her mind. After a few minutes, she found the ragged edges of her chafed nerves smoothing out.

A gull squawked overhead. Katie jumped. Her eyes flew open. Maybe her nerves weren't quite as placid as she'd thought.

Glancing at Grant standing beside her, looking obscenely handsome in a cream shirt and khaki shorts, she could almost forget that he'd blackmailed her into this trip—almost. The waves weren't *that* soothing, and she wasn't ready to forgive and forget just yet. Besides, being on an amiable plane with Grant posed emotional challenges she didn't want to face, now or ever.

Hitting a gentle swell, the boat rocked slightly, tipping her against Grant's arm. She glanced at him and took a small step closer to the boat's chrome railing to prevent a repeat of the contact. Trying to dismiss as her imagination the tingling racing down her arm from shoulder to fingertip, she grabbed the rail and raised her chin to inhale the fresh saltwater air. In the distance, she heard the muted clang of a bell.

Fastening her gaze on the bouncing bow of the

boat, she could just barely make out a large dark shape that seemed to materialize with their approach. She stiffened. Had Elmer, the Biddles' caretaker and the navigator of the boat, seen it also? The boat's throaty diesel engine being cut back to just above idle underscored Katie's reborn concern. Her fingers tightened on the railing to which she'd been clinging. "What's wrong? Are we stopping?"

"It's all right, dear." Harriet laid a calming hand on her arm. "We'll soon be coming into our little cove. Elmer grew up here and has fished these waters for over fifty years—he knows this area like the back of his hand. A little fog is nothing to him." Katie threw her hostess a skeptical look. "Trust me. He knows exactly where we are all the time."

Trust.

Gilligan and the castaways had trusted the Skipper and look where they'd ended up. She'd trusted Grant and look where it had gotten her—on a boat heading for a remote island to spend two weeks with the last man on earth she wanted to be near. And it didn't help that Grant seemed to have been born with sea legs. Without a seaworthy bone in her body, as long as she was on this island, she'd be just another bumbling Gilligan who, despite not having a clue, tried to keep pace with the others.

Katie crossed her arms over the bright turquoise blouse that matched her shorts, conscious of the dampness that had seeped into the material, and kept her gaze glued on the object ahead. Gradually, it began to take the blurry form of an island. Running her hand through her ever-tightening curls, she wished she'd had the sense to confine her hair in a barrette. She'd looked forward to the wind whipping it around her face. What she hadn't counted on was this infernal mist turning it into a large, red fuzzball.

Slowly, as they drew closer to land, as if by the wave of an unseen purveyor's hand, the wall of fog thinned. Shortly thereafter, the sun greeted them with the promise of a clear, warm day. Katie exhaled her relief.

Beside her, Harriet clapped her hands like a small schoolgirl and grinned. "I was so hoping the fog would lift before we actually got to the island. It's such an impressive sight from the ocean." Her gaze left Katie and shifted to beyond the bow of the boat.

Katie's gaze followed. She sucked in a surprised breath. "The cottage," as Harriet and Alfred had referred to their island home, but which Harriet had told her was officially known as The Homeplace, reigned over Windsor Island like a sedate monarch. Surrounded by spruce trees and sitting atop the highest point on the island, the Victorian-style white clapboard house gazed regally out over land, sea and sky. Colorful flower beds dotted the lawn sloping down to disappear behind a stand of the stately spruce trees. Tucked into a crescent-shaped inlet in the shoreline, another building stood beside a short dock jutting out into the small cove. The dock was piled with metal-mesh cratelike objects.

"Harriet, it's beautiful," Katie said, referring to

The Homeplace. "Have you furnished it authentically?"

"Yes. We were fortunate that when the house went up for sale, the owners left all the furniture. I kept most of the items and just added a touch here and there to make it ours." Pointing toward the turret on the west corner of the house, Harriet continued. "That turret is in the master bedroom and is original, but Alfred and I had skylights installed so we could lie in bed and look at the stars. Out here, without the interference of city lights, the heavens are magnificent, clear and dotted with thousands of twinkling stars." Her grin widened. She nudged Katie and winked. "Very romantic."

Romantic Katie didn't need. In fact, she'd already promised herself that anything remotely romantic would be given a wide berth. She wasn't about to get trapped in a situation from which she couldn't extract herself. She glanced at Grant, sprawled in a canvas deck chair at the back of the boat.

Grant observed Katie from his vantage point. He could hear her conversation with Harriet, but couldn't make out their exact words over the hum of the engine. That didn't bother him. He contented himself with getting reacquainted with Katie's shapely, tanned legs and how they seemed to go on forever, an advantage he hadn't had when he'd met her at college.

He grinned to himself, recalling how she'd seemed all clothes that first day. Covered from head to toe with a tie-died muslin sixties-style muumuu, Katie'd had very little flesh visible—except her inevitable bare feet. But when she'd turned those sparkling green eyes on him and his stomach had somersaulted to his knees, he'd known he was a dead man.

Back then, Katie had possessed an indomitable zest for life. What had happened to her? What had taken the freewheeling Katie and put her in a slot the old Katie would have fought tooth and nail? The old Katie would have sated her appetite for adventure on this whole situation, loving every minute of living on the edge of being discovered. This Katie worried and fretted and couldn't see beyond the confines of her new life.

Sitting up straight, Grant decided he wanted the old Katie back, if only for the duration of this trip. He vowed to himself to do everything in his power to make sure *his* Katie stuck the uptight woman she'd become in a drawer and left her there until they returned to Florida.

But first he had to get her to forgive him for blackmailing her, a little item that had him bathing in self-loathing.

Like a baby nestling into its mother's arms, the boat slipped in beside the dock, then bobbed on its own wake. Grant moved toward the cabin where they'd stowed their bags.

Harriet snagged his arm. "Elmer will bring up the bags. He has a golf cart and trailer in the storage shed just for that. Two things Alfred insisted on when we bought the house, besides modern bathrooms, was a golf cart and a boat that didn't smell like fish." She lowered her voice to whisper. "I can tell you it took Elmer some time to get used to this boat. I still don't think he likes driving it." Pointing to the opening in the chrome rail that provided a step to the dock, she chuckled lightly. "You two run along up to the house. We'll be right behind you just as soon as Alfred helps Elmer with the luggage."

"Are you sure I can't give them a hand?" Grant offered.

"No. You and Katie can leave that to us. Just run along and start enjoying your vacation." Harriet smiled knowingly at Katie.

"But—" Katie sputtered.

"Do as Harriet says," Alfred said, waving his hand as if shooing flies. He'd spent the entire trip on the flybridge with Elmer. It was the first either Grant or Katie had seen of him since they'd left the dock in Rockland. "We'll catch up. Just go through the boat-house, then follow the path through the spruce trees. It'll bring you to the south patio."

Reluctantly, Grant climbed onto the built-in step, then onto the floating dock. He turned and extended his arms to aid Katie. She glared at him, then, ignoring his offer of help, she pivoted her weight to step to the dock. Her foot slipped, launching her over the side at Grant.

To prevent her from being catapulted into the water, Grant caught her and clutched her to his chest. Ribbons of sensation chased each other up and down his body. Katie might have changed, but the effect she had on his libido hadn't. Instantly, he loosened his hold. At the same moment, Katie pushed him away.

"What the hell…" Frantically, Grant fought to maintain his precarious balance on the edge of the dock. He lost the battle.

Icy water closed over his head. Salt water infiltrated his windpipe and seared its way to his lungs. Pushing off the bottom, he swam back to the surface.

Gasping for air and choking, he threw his wet hair out of his way with a toss of his head, then gazed up to find four faces staring down at him. Harriet's and Alfred's showed genuine concern for his well-being. Elmer shook his head and walked away.

Then there was Katie.

"Oops." A glimmer of satisfaction and that impish grin he recalled so well spread over her face.

So, the old Katie still existed inside that starched shell she showed the world. He grinned back at her. Deep inside, he knew he'd found the road to her forgiveness.

"YOU DID that on purpose."

Katie glanced at Grant walking beside her up the dirt path to the cottage.

"Did not." She fought to keep a straight face.

Grant's hair, except for that inevitable stray wave hanging over his eyebrow, dripped down the neck of his shirt. His clothes, once pristine and straight out of L.L. Bean, carried scars of his dunking in the cove. He plucked at the material clinging to him everywhere. On one hip, a piece of brown seaweed had attached itself. Tempted to pick it off and toss it into the weeds bordering the path, she decided against it.

A disheveled Grant proved safer to her senses than the spit-and-polished man who'd sat next to her on the plane. He'd been far too handsome all morning. His drenched state gave her perspective, a breather from the emotions he'd been bringing to life in her. Emotions she hadn't felt for over seven years. Emotions Charles hadn't even touched.

No. She had to stop thinking like that. Charles was the only man for her.

Then Grant turned to her and smiled. He could have been wearing rags and smelling like a swamp and she couldn't have turned off the overwhelming response her body experienced.

Damn him!

She didn't want to see him as anything but a pain in her— She didn't want to like him. She didn't want to feel this magnetic pull for him. Why didn't her body understand that?

She was engaged to Charles. She had no business wanting to throw herself in Grant's arms every time he smiled at her.

"Katie, you pushed me into the water on purpose. Admit it."

"Don't be childish. Of course I didn't do it on purpose. Why would I?" Rather than look him in the eye, Katie busied herself taking in the towering spruce tress and the smell of ocean air that clung to the fresh breeze cooling her heated cheeks.

He stopped walking and took her by the shoulders. "Because sometimes, that starched Katie you show the world can't control the Katie I used to know. The Katie who took delight in wading through the fountain under the dean's window. The Katie who would rather die than wear shoes. The Katie who would have looked at this whole situation through laughter and the excitement of adventure."

Tearing her shoulders away from his grip, Katie huffed and turned away. "Adventure? No, Grant. Not even the old Katie, were she still alive and kicking, would have found this mess you've gotten us into an adventure. Funny perhaps. Lord knows, if I couldn't find humor in all this, I'd do something desperate—" she cast a glance at him "—like strangle you where you stand."

He caught up with her. "Okay, so maybe it isn't an adventure, but we're in this together. We have to make peace or the Biddles are never going to believe we're happily married."

Katie threw up her hands and faced him. "Oh yes, we're back to your job. Heaven forbid we endanger your promotion."

Suddenly, she became very tired of being angry, of fighting with Grant. It was done. They were going to spend two weeks with each other and there wasn't anything either of them could do about it. They might as well call a truce.

She raised her gaze to meet his. "Okay, Grant. We'll muck through this somehow."

He smiled again.

Damn him!

Her stomach flopped and her body got all warm and mushy. His gaze captured hers in its depths and held her against her will. The roar of the waves crashing against the rocks died to a murmur. The screeching gulls suddenly became mute. The wind caressed her face like a lover's hand. Her body swayed toward his. Her gaze shifted to his mouth, the same mouth that had once kissed her senseless.

"Well, you two haven't made much progress."

Harriet's voice cut through the heady emotions blanketing Grant and Katie. Katie sprang away, her gaze searching for something to fasten on. In the distance, a small island with a lighthouse on its tip had appeared out of the fog.

"Is that yours, Harriet?" Katie stepped past Grant and pointed at the island.

"Yes. It's called Little Windsor and came with the big island." Although directed at his wife, Alfred answered Katie's question.

"I'm afraid there's not much there besides the lighthouse and a few dozen gray seals sunning themselves," Harriet added, then dismissed it and made her way a few feet up the path before turning to them.

"I'd love to see it. Is there a way out there?" Katie kept stride with Harriet.

"You can reach it in a skiff. Elmer has one he can loan you."

"Oh, I'm afraid I'm not much with boats." Katie smiled apologetically. After the trip over here, she felt a little foolish drawing still more attention to her lack of nautical know-how.

"Well, Grant can take you. You certainly wouldn't want to go without him, would you?"

What had she gotten herself into? "Maybe it isn't such a good idea."

"Nonsense. You'd love it. Solitude. Communing with nature." Harriet gave a short, decisive nod of her head. "I'll pack a picnic so the two of you can go tomorrow. Now, come along. We need to get you settled in your room so poor Grant can dry off." Moving ahead of them, she made her way toward the large house peeking through the branches of the trees.

Their room. Stunned into silence, Katie forgot the picnic instantly. Lord, she'd never given a thought to the sleeping accommodations. The Biddles thought they were married. On top of everything else, she'd be sharing a bedroom with Grant Waverly.

"Gonna be an interesting couple of weeks," Grant muttered as he fell into step with her. Indisputable humor tinged his voice.

"Neanderthal." Katie increased her speed to catch up with Harriet. Did men ever think of anything besides sex?

ALTHOUGH HE'D made light of it, Harriet's reminder about the sleeping accommodations he and Katie would be sharing had rattled Grant right down to his fancy deck shoes. The thought of sharing a bed with Katie had his hormones launching into an explosion that would rival Fourth of July fireworks.

He shook himself. What was he thinking? He was here to secure his future at the firm, nothing more. When the two weeks ended, he'd return Katie to Charles. Period. Good grief, he was an adult. As such, he could control his emotions for fourteen days.

Couldn't he?

THE HOMEPLACE looked like a white gingerbread house. Katie couldn't believe the size of the place, nor the beauty. It seemed to sprawl across the highest point of the island, taking its fair share out of the fifteen acres, while at the same time nestling down into the arms of a rose garden alive with color and scent. A porch stretched the full length of the house, affording a panoramic view of the ocean.

"Come along," Harriet called, leading her little entourage through the double oak doors. "Plenty of time for sight-seeing later. Grant needs to get dry. We'll have coffee on the patio in an hour, and you can enjoy the view to your heart's content." She ushered them into the large foyer. Without missing a step, she headed straight up the stairs. "Elmer will have your clothes up here very soon. In the meantime, Grant, you take a nice hot shower."

Half listening, Katie trailed Harriet and Grant up the winding staircase, trying to take in the antiques that abounded inside the house. Sideboards, Chippendale chairs, gilded picture frames made up only a small portion of what she saw. As she moved onto the upstairs landing, she glanced inside one of the open bedroom doors. Twin beds. Hoping against hope, she took a step in that direction.

"No, dear. That's my grandchildren's room. You and Grant will be staying in here." With a flourish, Harriet swept open the door to the room across the hall.

Katie sidled past her. Grant followed. They caught their breath simultaneously. Harriet had brought them into the master bedroom, complete with skylights and turret. "But, Harriet, this is your room. We couldn't—"

"Nonsense. Alfred and I have made up our minds. You two lovebirds will stay here and Alfred and I will take the north bedroom. It'll be like a second honeymoon."

Honeymoon?

Grant swallowed hard. One look at this room and he knew he'd be in big trouble if he stayed here. Grant stepped forward, wondering if Alfred really had anything to do with the decision. "Harriet, this is too much to ask of you."

"Tut-tut." Harriet swept around the room, opening windows and whisking away imaginary specks of dust from the furniture. "We won't take no for an answer. This room will be yours for the length of your stay…oh, dear, the girl who comes in to remove the dustcovers forgot to give you an extra blanket…well, poor thing, her mother's been ill, you know, arthritis, and the poor child has to take care of her, their house, and all the houses she opens for the summer visitors…it's just so much to ask of such a little thing…she's no more than a snip of a girl…I'll get you another blanket after dinner…Grant, do get in the shower, dear boy.''

Grant looked to Katie for help. She shrugged helplessly. "Harriet, I—"

"Grant, dear, stop sputtering and get out of those wet clothes…you'll be catching your death…I'll get Elmer up here with your luggage straightaway." She spun toward the door and opened it. "Make yourselves at home." And, like a wisp of smoke, she was gone.

"Leaves you a bit breathless, doesn't she?" When he got no reply, Grant looked at Katie. She hadn't heard a word he'd said. Her fixed gaze scanned the turret and the king-size bed nestled inside a curved bank of windows overlooking the ocean. Through the three skylights above it, sun and blue sky canopied the bed. Oh, this was dangerous territory all right.

Looking around the room, Grant spotted two sofas positioned in front of a fireplace. Cozy! Romance seemed to abound in every corner of the room. He never would have believed his staid boss would permit such quixotic surroundings. But when Harriet got wound up, Alfred had already proven himself to be as helpless against her as Grant was.

"I can't do this."

Katie's frantic whisper startled him into awareness. "Do what?"

"Share this…this…harem room with you." Suddenly, she whirled on him. "You did this, didn't you?

It's your weird sense of humor raising its ugly little head.''

Baffled, he frowned at her. "What? What did I do?''

"This." She waved her arm in a wide arc, encompassing the entire room. "All this. You arranged with Harriet to give us this room.''

"Katie, something's eating your brain. Why on earth would I make sure that I spent two weeks sleeping in one of the most romantic rooms I have ever seen with a woman who can't stand the sight of me?"

She ignored him or didn't hear him because she was too busy tearing bedding from the bed and transferring it to one of the sofas. "Just in case you have any cute ideas, you'll be sleeping there," she announced, tossing one of the bed pillows on top of the pile.

"Aren't you going to draw a line down the middle of the room and tell me to stay on my own side?" He couldn't stop the grin that curved his lips.

Katie glared at him. The man knew exactly when to turn that smile on. Just when she'd worked up a good head of steam, he turned off her heat. Well, he could grin until his face split open. He was not sleeping with her in that...that... She couldn't find the word, but it certainly wasn't *bed*. Not with that glass roof and all those windows and the sound of the ocean crashing against the rocks at the bottom of the rocky ledge. Scandalous! That's what it was. An aphrodisiac. A blatant enticement to make love.

And, heaven help her, she wanted to... To what?

Share it with him? Lose herself in his arms the way she had when they were in the back seat of his car at college? Experience again the passion that she'd tasted so long ago? What did she want?

She wanted Grant Waverly out of her sight. "Go take a shower."

Grant threw up his hands. "Why is it everyone is so concerned about my hygiene?"

Against her will, a giggle escaped Katie. "Maybe because you smell like seaweed?"

Grant looked down at himself. He picked the seaweed off his hip and curled his nose. Throwing her an apologetic look, he headed for the bathroom. "When my clothes get here, would you find me a pair of jeans and a shirt?" he called over his shoulder.

She glared at his retreating back, then shook her head. "Okay."

The bathroom door closed behind him, and Katie immediately regretted agreeing. Picking out Grant's clothes was so…so intimate…so domestic. Oh, hell, wasn't she supposed to be playing the loving wife for two weeks? She might just as well start now.

To keep her hands busy and her traitorous mind occupied, she made up the bed for Grant on the couch. Then she realized if Harriet should come back, she'd undoubtedly wonder. Katie removed the bedding she'd tossed there earlier, folded it, then laid it on the end of the bed.

Katie was just about to explore the staircase leading toward the roof at the side of the turret when a knock sounded on the door. Opening it, she came face-to-face with the wizened, ruddy-faced man who'd piloted the boat to the island. Loaded down with luggage, Elmer sidestepped her and walked to the center of the room. He deposited the bags in a heap, then straightened.

"Thanks, Mr...." She waited for him to fill in the blank, which he didn't seem in any hurry to do.

"Coffin. Folks 'round here just call me Elmer."

Coffin?

Gratitude at not having been aware of the full name of the man who'd navigated them across miles of deep, cold ocean drained Katie's legs of strength. She sank to the dressing table stool. "Is that all of them?" she asked in a weakened tone.

"Ayuh."

Without another word, Elmer turned and left the room, leaving the door standing ajar behind him. Summoning her strength, Katie rose, then closed the door. Turning, she faced the stack of luggage and mentally picked out those bags that belonged to Grant. Selecting the larger one, she threw it on the bed and snapped the catches open.

Inside, she was greeted by stacks of clothes—Grant's clothes. Her mind went berserk with thoughts of them covering Grant's muscular body, caressing his skin, absorbing his scent.

Hell's bells! If she didn't stop this daydreaming, she'd be a basket case at the end of the first day. Angrily, she looked at the bathroom door. Beyond it she could hear the sound of rushing water. Again, her mind took a side trip to muse about Grant taking a shower.

Decisively, she dragged her gaze from the door and centered all her attention on finding clothes for Grant as she'd promised. Cautiously, she fingered a pair of white jockey shorts. Her skin temperature rose several degrees. She dropped them as if they'd burned her.

It was no use. She couldn't do this. And he knew it. He was probably standing behind that door laughing himself silly with visions of her trying to pick out his clothes, handling his underwear and entertaining memories of their college romance.

Without a second thought, she grabbed the suitcase and turned it upside down in the middle of the bed. Throwing it aside, she grabbed the next one and did the same. A few minutes latter, she had emptied the contents of three suitcases, one shoe bag and a garment bag on the bed.

"There you go," she told the bathroom door. "All laid out. Just take your pick."

Dusting her hands off, she smirked at the door one last time, then strode out of the room. Maybe she could come up with some story to tell Harriet that would make it possible to put Grant in another room. Her mood brightened at the prospect of not having to spend the night listening to Grant sleeping not twelve feet from her.

"If I get him out of the room, I just might be able to make it through these next two weeks. If not—"

She applied the brakes to those thoughts. She didn't even want to consider what would happen in this setting with a man she had to fight to resist—even in her mind.

As she reached the foot of the curved staircase, Harriet rounded the corner of the dining room, her arms loaded with navy bath towels.

"I was just bringing these up to Grant. I found them in the laundry room, which means there are no towels in your bathroom." She handed the pile to Katie. "Would you be a dear and run these upstairs for me? I'm trying to get dinner started. Thanks." And, in her usual Harriet fashion, she was gone.

Katie stared down at the towels, then glanced up the stairs. Shrugging, she retraced her steps to the master bedroom. Opening the door, she stepped over the threshold—and came to a screeching halt.

On the bed, concealed to his waist by the pile of clothing she'd dumped from his suitcase, sat Grant—in the buff.

Chapter Six

Grant hiked up the navy-blue bath mat he clutched around the lower half of his body. "Thanks for laying out my clothes."

He realized his weak attempt at sarcasm was lost behind the smile he felt creep over his lips. Actually, he'd laughed when he'd found the pile of clothes. The old Katie had paid another visit.

Speechless, Katie continued to gape at him from the other side of the room, clasping a pile of towels, her eyes resembling those of a deer caught in a car's high beams.

He pointed at the pile of terry cloth in Katie's arms. "Are they the missing towels?"

She looked down at her burden, as if realizing for the first time what she held, then nodded. "Uh-huh."

"May I have one?"

She blinked. "Oh! Yes...sure. Here." She extended the pile to him, keeping her distance on the other side of the room.

Grant glanced down at his meager covering, then back to her. "Katie, do you really want me to come over there to get one?" He grinned. "Exhibitionist has never been one of my life's aspirations."

The second the words passed his lips, he could have bitten off his tongue.

Her expression changed instantly from one of bemusement to one of anger. "No. We both know what you aspired to and it wasn't as simple as a dry towel or—" She cut off her words between tightly pursed lips. Kathleen Donovan was back. Without another word, she strode forward, thrust the towels at him, then turned and left the room.

Nice going, Waverly. How do you expect to present a good front for your boss if the woman who's supposed to be in love with you keeps walking away?

Katie walking away.

Boy, did that resurrect some memories he'd rather not contend with at the moment. Taking the pile of towels into the bathroom, he pushed away the nagging memories of that cold day in the parking lot of the college campus. He didn't want to think about what he was quickly coming to see as the biggest mistake of his life. He had more important things to consider than events that he could not alter, even if he wanted to. The promotion. He must concentrate on the promotion.

"I'LL MAKE SURE I pack a picnic lunch for you and Grant to take over to Little Windsor tomorrow. You can spend the day exploring the ruins of the light keeper's cottage and the old lighthouse." Harriet stacked the dirty plates. "You might not want to try swimming. Aside from the rocks and the strong undertow, the water temperatures are quite a bit colder than those we enjoy in Florida.'' She disappeared with the dishes around the kitchen counter.

''Are you sure I can't help?'' Katie called after her, feeling like a freeloader.

She didn't want to think about spending a day alone with Grant. In fact, she didn't want to think about Grant at all. Especially after seeing him in nothing but a bath mat. The thoughts that had rampaged through her head still had the power to make her cheeks burn.

''No. It'll only take me a minute to fill the dishwasher, then I'll bring out the coffee.'' Harriet eyed Katie through the opening from the kitchen. ''You're looking a bit warm, dear. Why don't you join Alfred and Grant on the deck? It's much cooler out there.''

Because of the lateness of the hour, they'd opted for a light supper of salad and sandwiches in the breakfast nook, rather than the formal dining room. Through the window, Katie could see Seal Light's rhythmic beam flashing from Little Windsor. There had been a time in her life when she'd have given all she owned to be marooned on a deserted island with Grant. But not now. Not when her entire body begged her to take advantage of Harriet's picnic.

Charles. She had to think about Charles.

She closed her eyes and tried to visualize the face of the man who would be her husband in three months, but another face kept intruding.

"I think I will go outside, maybe take a walk." Standing, she made her way to the deck.

Grant sat atop the wide board railing encircling the deck. Alfred lounged in a deck chair. Katie smiled to herself, thinking that no matter what Alfred wore, no matter where he sat, he still looked as if he resided at the head of a board table, conducting legal business. Probably what Grant would look like in years to come. The epitome of an executive.

"Katie, would you like to sit here?" Alfred rose, offering her his chair. "I'm afraid Elmer didn't get all the outdoor furniture out. Short notice and all." Grant's staid boss emitted a rare chuckle. "It's his way of paying us back for not providing him with the agreed upon month to get things ready for our stay. I'm afraid he's very set in his ways. It wouldn't surprise me if he got them out, then put them back just to be contrary. Cantankerous old..."

Katie glanced to where Grant watched her. She couldn't sit here and let him stare at her like a manikin in a store window. "Thanks, but I think I'll take a walk and work off the pie I had for desert."

Grant slipped off his perch. "Want some company?"

She shook her head. "No. Thanks. I think I'd just like some time alone to absorb the peace of the night." Once she and Grant retired to that room upstairs, there would be little peace for her.

Shrugging, Grant hoisted himself back atop the railing. "Suit yourself."

She took a step off the deck.

"Katie?"

She turned back to face Grant. "Yes?"

"Wish on a star for me."

Katie's heart thumped loud in her ears. For a minute she saw the old Grant in his eyes, the Grant who said those words to her every night when he dropped her off at her dorm. Back then their wishes had been alike, or so she'd believed, and she could have wished for both of them.

Then reality set in. Now, like then, she knew the only wish Grant had was for that corner office looking out on the Miami skyline and a nameplate and key to the executive washroom. Nowhere in that picture was there room for Katie Donovan—even if she wanted to be part of it. Which she didn't.

"Maybe you better make your own wishes." She hurried into the darkness before he could see the moisture running down her cheeks.

Grant's gaze followed Katie's progress across the moonlit lawn until she disappeared into the inky shadows of some tall spruce trees. He had no idea what had made him say that. Nostalgia maybe. Maybe just a simple wish that he could go back to those college days and make things right for her. Deep inside, he felt partially responsible for the disappearance of the old Katie Donovan, the Katie who smiled easy and laughed often. The Katie who had loved him and filled him with a zest for living.

"So tell me, Grant, do you foresee any trouble negotiating the contract with the government?"

Alfred's words jolted Grant from his reverie. He

had to think for a second. "Ah...no, I don't see any problems, sir." For once, he didn't want to talk law. His mind had followed Katie into the shadows.

"Alfred. Call me Alfred, my boy."

Grant smiled and nodded. "Putnam has already made it clear that he has certain ideas about how he'll operate and the government seems quite happy with his stipulations. Unless one of them has an abrupt change of heart, everything should go very smoothly."

Alfred flattened a wrinkle in his khaki trousers, then smiled. "That's why I want you as one of the juniors, Grant. You know your clients. Aside from being able to give them top legal representation, you've gotten inside their heads and can predict trouble before it happens. I like that."

"I did not come all the way from Florida to spend two weeks listening to you two talk shop." Harriet emerged from the sliding glass doors leading from the breakfast nook onto the deck. In her hands she carried a tray bearing four cups and a carafe. "There will be no more mention of cases or law firms for the duration of our vacation." She glanced around. "Where's Katie?"

"She went for a walk in the moonlight." Alfred rose and took the tray from his wife. Looking around, he huffed impatiently. "Elmer never brought out the table."

"Stop fussing and put the tray on the floor, Alfred." Harriet moved the chair back to make a space. "Grant, why ever did you let Katie go alone? There's nothing more unromantic than walking alone on a lovely moonlit night.''

''She didn't seem to want company.'' In fact, Grant had the distinct impression that, had he pushed the subject, she would have found any number of excuses to go alone. Grant squatted beside the tray, then poured coffee into three of the earthenware mugs. He handed one to Harriet.

''Nonsense. Women want to be coaxed,'' Harriet said, slipping into the chair Alfred vacated for her. In the process, her spoon slipped to the floor. ''Oh, dear.''

Alfred leaned down to retrieve it. ''For goodness sake, Harriet, give it a rest. You're acting as if you're Cupid's first in command. These two young people can solve their own problems with no stage setting from you.''

Alfred's whispered aside to his wife was not lost to Grant. He pretended as if he hadn't heard, but his mind came alive with possible explanations for their comments. Why would Harriet be playing Cupid? He thought he and Katie had been handling things quite well. What could have caused Harriet to think that his and Katie's marriage was in some kind of trouble? Now that he thought about it, she'd certainly been pushing the romance angle ever since they'd boarded the plane for Maine. Then there was the bedroom.

Well, just to make certain, he'd let Katie know that they had to redouble their efforts to convince the Biddles that his and Katie's marriage was sound and happy. That would mean burying this hatchet that had hung between them since college days. Considering Katie's attitude every time he mentioned college, this would be no easy task. But if he wanted that junior partnership, they would have to present a solid matrimonial front.

A solid matrimonial front meant a whole lot more than sharing a bedroom. They'd have to convey, through their actions, that they were in love and happy about it. It was going to take some fancy acting on their parts. Well, on Katie's part. Grant was slowly beginning to realize that, where Katie Donovan was concerned, he couldn't ignore the constant eruption of his emotions and the resurgence of some very old feelings.

KATIE AMBLED into the dimly lit family room to find Grant staring thoughtfully into a blazing hearth. She wrapped her arms around herself, absorbing the warmth.

"That damp sea air really goes to the bone. Especially with that breeze." She moved to the raised hearth and sat.

"You've been gone a long time."

"I walked along the beach, then sat on a rock and watched the light from the lighthouse go 'round and 'round. It's like a fire. Mesmerizing." She glanced around, suddenly realizing they were alone. "Where're Harriet and Alfred?"

Grant smiled and leaned forward, resting his elbows on his knees. "They went to bed. Harriet said when you came back, we'd probably want some time alone.''

Katie stared at him for a moment, feeling the resurgence of the emotions she'd been grappling with all day. She tore her gaze from his and stared into the leaping crimson-and-orange flames spiraling up from the sweet-scented pine logs.

She really needed to get a grip on this whole situation. She had to consider Charles and their future together. But how, when she hadn't come to terms with her past, could she plan a future?

"Katie, we need to talk."

Grant's tone drew her gaze back to his. *Not again.* Unlike the time on the porch, his expression showed concern and the shadow of trouble.

Her mind flew to her mother. Could something have happened to Lizzie? "What's wrong? Is it my mother?"

Grant shook his head. "No. It's nothing like that." He paused, as if unwilling to go on. "It's about us."

"Us?"

"Harriet and Alfred think our marriage is in trouble. That's why Harriet's been doing her utmost to push us into every romantic setting she can find." He glanced at Katie's face, waiting for the explosion. None came. "I know this is not something you want to do, but I'd appreciate it if you would help me prove to them that we have a strong, loving marriage by openly appearing like a loving couple."

"I thought we'd already been doing that. I'm here, acting the devoted wife."

Standing, Grant came to sit beside her on the hearth. Heat from the fire burned into his back, but nothing like the fire building inside him for Katie. "That's not enough. We need to…to *act* loving, to *show* them that we're in love."

Katie stiffened. "And how do you propose we do that?"

Running his hand through his hair, Grant searched for the right words. "By holding hands, cuddling, kissing from time to time." When he saw her expression turn stubborn, he held up his hand. "Nothing deep and soul-searching, just a peck here and there."

"Well, I suppose that wouldn't hurt. But don't get any ideas about it going any further than pretense."

Grant caught her gaze for a moment, wondering if she was speaking to him or herself. Before he could say more, she rose and retreated to the couch. "You're always walking away from me, Katie Donovan. Why do you suppose that is?"

Katie looked past him, into the crackling flames of the hearth. "I wasn't the first to walk away. Just the first to do it physically."

This conversation had taken a turn into dangerous territory. Katie wanted to go to bed, but would Grant follow? She wasn't ready to share that room at the top of the stairs with him just yet. She wasn't sure she'd ever be ready for that.

"I never walked away from you." His low voice came from beside her. When had he moved?

Uncomfortable with his nearness, Katie edged closer to her end of the couch, leaving a space between them. "Then what would you call it? Why did you agree to go through with that fake wedding ceremony?"

"Because we'd all had too many beers and wanted to live a little crazy. Because that old man was willing to perform it." He paused, then looked straight at her. "Because you wanted to do it."

"But did you?" She wanted to stop this conversation before it got to the parts that would bring the old pain to the surface where she could no longer ignore it, but she'd waited too long for the explanations that had never come that day in the parking lot. No matter how much it hurt, she had to know. "Did you ever really love me, Grant?"

"Of course I loved you. How can you doubt that?"

"Did you want that ceremony to be real as much as I did?"

Grant reached for her, but she stood and began pacing the space in front of the fireplace. "Did you ever love me more than your career?"

Bowing his head in his hands, Grant breathed a sigh. "Katie, I tried to explain back then but you refused to understand."

"No. You didn't. You never tried. You just said it might be years before we could start a home and family." Suddenly, having Grant explain this became vital to her. This was the closest he'd ever come to opening up to her. Kneeling in front of him, she placed her hand on his arm and gazed directly into his eyes. "I want to understand. Talk to me."

Grant stared at her for a long moment, wondering

what words he could say that he hadn't already said to make her see why they'd had to wait. "I worked my way through college, Katie. My parents were not rich people."

"They weren't poor, either. I met them over the Thanksgiving recess, remember? They're average working people."

"Who lived paycheck to paycheck. They never had an extra cent for anything."

She sat back on her heels and shook her head. "But they had love. Your father was there every night to tuck you in. Isn't that more important than money and position?"

What she said sounded good, but Grant had lived with the reality. Memories of all the things he'd had to do without buffeted Grant's mind. He began poking at the fire with one of the brass tools to escape them, but they couldn't be held at bay that easily.

School outings he'd missed, because the rent had to be paid. Toys his friends had but he couldn't get, because a car payment had come due. A secondhand bike, because his parents couldn't afford the one he'd wanted in Jamison's store window.

"My parents struggled to pay bills, struggled to keep a roof over our heads, struggled to put clothes on my back. I will not subject my wife and children to that kind of life." He turned to face her. "I worked damned hard to put myself through law school. Although I love what I do now, I had no burning desire to be a lawyer. I wanted it only because it would provide a good living, one I could share with my family someday.''

Katie stood. ''Hopefully, that struggle made you a better person.''

''Oh, it did. Your problem, Katie, is that you always thought with your heart and not your head. I worked for everything I got. I have nothing to be sorry for.''

''Nothing?''

He could see the pain in her face, but he could not deny it. He hated that she hadn't been able to wait until he felt he could give a good home to her and their children. He didn't regret working to become the best lawyer around. His only regret was that he'd lost her in the process.

Katie laughed mirthlessly. ''Funny thing is, you had something very precious that you didn't have to work for, but you threw it away.''

He shook his head. Katie recognized the stubborn tilt of his head. Even now, he was unwilling to see that he'd made the wrong decisions back then. ''If I had it to do all over again, I'd do nothing differently.''

The pain came then, hard and sharp. She'd known it would, but somehow, she hadn't expected it to still have the power to slice through her heart like a knife. Time had not dulled the edge one bit. She took a deep breath. She still didn't understand how a man could put career before the woman he was supposed to love and a life with her—just like her father had.

''How do you suppose we ended up really married?'' Her voice sounded thin and tired to her ears. She cleared her throat. ''I mean, the minister knew it was just a joke, didn't he?'' She set a smile on her lips, then turned toward him. ''Maybe it was because he was a mail-order minister.'' Hell, if she didn't laugh about all this, she'd run screaming from the room.

His gaze fixed on her. ''I'm not sure how it happened. I know that getting his license out of the back of a *Field and Stream* for tax purposes didn't make him any less official. Someone just slipped up, or he didn't understand about the pretense part. Thinking back on it, I'm wondering who'd had more to drink, him or us.''

Laughing nervously, Katie sank down on the hearth and took up Grant's abandoned poker. Grant came to sit beside her. The fire had started to die and the warmth was more like a gentle caress on her shoulders than the searing heat of before.

''I seem to recall that he had a difficult time balancing himself on that little box he insisted on standing on to perform the ceremony.'' Getting caught up in the happy memories, Katie smiled with real humor. ''If it hadn't been for our friends propping him up, he never would have made it through the whole thing.''

Grant snickered. ''Remember when he pitched backward and his toupee slipped over his eyes?''

Katie dropped the poker and began to laugh. ''You said that it looked as if he had a cat sleeping on his forehead.'' Katie's strung-out nerves fed her uncontrollable laughter. Tears cascaded down her cheeks. She slipped off the hearth and crumpled into a pile on the Oriental carpeting.

Before long, she felt Grant slide down next to her. Glancing sideways, through her tears, she could see him leaning against the hearth and holding his sides. His face was contorted in silent laughter. "And remember the toast he made after?" He straightened and held his hand out as if he held a glass. "'To the happy couple…hic…may they alwaysh…be…' Then he faded away and passed out cold."

Katie's laughter stopped abruptly. "I wonder what he was going to say."

"Probably that we'd always be happy." Grant's laughter had stopped, too.

He'd turned toward her, his expression one Katie didn't want to understand. She brushed a wave of dark hair off his forehead. He caught her hand and kissed her fingertips.

"We were happy, weren't we, my Katie?"

The familiar endearment stirred emotions she'd fought valiantly to keep safely in her past. "Yes, we were. For a while."

"What happened?"

She shook her head. Not because she didn't know the answer, but because saying it wouldn't solve anything. It would still be there, and she'd still resent his choice of a career over a life with her.

"Katie, I—" He stopped abruptly and leaned toward her, his gaze locked on her mouth.

She knew what she was going to do. She tried to

pull away, but she couldn't, couldn't deny the feelings she'd been experiencing since she'd seen him standing on her porch. Her heart spurred her on, drowning out the cries of her conscience. She wanted Grant's mouth on hers as much as she wanted to go on living. As much as she wanted the sun to come up tomorrow. As much as she knew it was wrong.

When Grant's lips covered hers for the first time in seven years, Katie felt her whole body come alive in a way that it hadn't for so long. Her blood hummed through her veins, making every nerve supersensitive to every pore in her skin. Her mind ceased to function, giving over to her emotions all the energy it took to think.

When Katie moaned deep in her throat, Grant's senses vibrated in response. He hadn't felt like this since…since that last time he'd held Katie and kissed her lips. She responded like no other woman ever could, with every fiber of her soul. He wondered if she reacted to what's-his-name like this.

The thought had the same effect as a dash of cold water in his face. Grant pulled away, reminding himself he'd been about to take advantage of another man's woman. Quickly, he stood, then ran his fingers through his hair, trying to catch his breath.

"I'm so sorry, Katie. That never should have happened." He glanced at her. She was staring fixedly at her hands folded in her lap. "Katie?"

"It's all right, Grant. I was as much to blame for that as you were. I could have stopped you and didn't."

He turned toward her and touched her hair with the tips of his fingers. "Why didn't you?"

She shook her head, glanced up at him, then stood and moved around him as if he had some communicable disease. "Let's not rationalize it to death. It happened. It shouldn't have. It won't happen again." She kept her face turned from him and walked toward the stairs leading out of the sunken family room and into the hall. "I'm going to bed. I'd appreciate it if you'd give me a few minutes before you come up."

He nodded, but she never saw it. By that time, she was already in the hall and starting up the stairs. Grant watched her disappear. Once again, she was walking away.

Flopping down on the hearth, he buried his face in his hands. Memories cascaded around him, memories of three years of loving and being loved by Katie. From out of those memories came the vision of her looking up at him with large trusting eyes full of love during the staged wedding ceremony. When had he lost that trust?

KATIE LAY LOOKING through one of the skylights at the stars twinkling above her. Under different circumstances, she could see this being the romantic experience Harriet had said it was. But the cold, empty bed held nothing but pain and recriminations for the kiss she'd shared with Grant.

Her reaction to that kiss had shocked her, unnerved her and had brought forward a whole new set of doubts and problems. Could she still marry Charles knowing what effect another man's kiss had on her? Could she go to him as his bride and remove that kiss from her mind?

The door opened. Katie closed her eyes. She didn't want to talk to Grant anymore that night. Too many questions still rushed through her mind. She needed to find answers. Answers to the feelings she was experiencing. Answers to the questions of her loyalty to one man and her need for another. Answers that remained annoyingly elusive. Suddenly, she knew what she had to do.

Quietly, she waited. When Grant had been in his makeshift bed on the couch for almost an hour, and she could hear the regular sound of his breathing, she slipped from the bed. Donning her robe and slippers, she crept out the door.

Downstairs, she checked the clock. It was not all that late. Charles would probably be awake correcting test papers. Making her way to the kitchen, she reached for the wall phone, dialed and leaned against the counter while she waited for her call to connect to Florida.

"Yes?" Charles sounded tired and preoccupied.

"Charles?"

"Katie." She could hear him shuffling papers. "Why didn't you call earlier? I've been waiting and worrying."

"I'm sorry. We got busy with dinner, then I went for a walk on the beach."

"Alone?" His voice had become crisp. The tone she hated.

"Yes, alone. Exactly who did you think I'd go with, Charles?"

A heavy sigh came through the receiver. "Forgive me. I've had a bull of a day. Two of my classes were canceled due to a small fire in the west wing. Then if that wasn't enough—"

"Charles." She didn't want to hear about fires or school or anything else. She needed to tell him something. "We need to talk."

"What is it?" His voice became instantly alert. "Is that Grant person behaving? If he isn't, you just say the word, and I'll come get you." She could imagine his posture stiffening along with his tone.

The silence at her end dragged on. Katie tried, but she couldn't seem to find the words to fill it.

"Katie, are you still there?"

"Yes, I'm here."

"What is it that you need to talk about? Is it him?"

How did she tell Charles that Grant was not the problem? Not really. The problem lay entirely with her. She couldn't control her emotions around a man she claimed to have gotten over seven years ago.

"Charles, I think we need to give our wedding some serious consideration."

"Oh dear, you haven't changed your mind about the arrangements again, have you? Katie, we can't keep moving the reception around. There just aren't enough places to—"

"No." She looked around guiltily, then lowered her voice. "No. It's not the arrangements. They're fine."

His long sigh of relief came through the phone. "Well, I'm certainly glad to hear that. You gave me a start...." His voice faded away. She could visualize him sitting ramrod straight in his desk chair, holding the phone to his ear and reading the next paper on the stack he was correcting, half listening to her.

"I don't want to talk about arrangements. I want to postpone the wedding."

The silence on the other end of the line dragged out for interminable seconds. She glanced at the ceiling for divine intervention. She waited. Still no sound. "Charles?"

More silence.

"Charles, speak to me."

"What am I to say?"

He sounded hurt. The last thing she wanted to do was hurt Charles. But she'd hurt him more if she didn't stop the wedding until she could be sure of her emotions. Wouldn't she? If they went ahead with their plans, they could easily end up in a divorce court like her mother.

Her mother!

Oh, wouldn't Lizzie lap this up like a hungry kitten, then shower her with I-told-you-sos?

"I'd really appreciate it if you didn't mention this to Mother." The last thing she needed was Lizzie gloating.

"I hardly think I'll go running to your mother with the news that her daughter jilted me. We both know I'm not her favorite candidate for son-in-law."

Katie sighed. She refused to go there. "I'm not

jilting you. I just think it's best if we call things off for a while. I need time to think.''

"Time to think? Four years wasn't long enough? How long do you expect me to sit around waiting for you? And if you aren't jilting me, what do you call going from postponing the wedding to calling it off?''

"I don't call it jilting you. I call it asking you to be a little patient while I work through some problems.''

"Problems? You didn't have any problems when you left here. Why all of a sudden do you have problems?''

This time the silence came from Katie's end of the phone. How could she explain that, since she'd been in Grant's company, her whole being seemed to have undergone a change? How could she tell him that she could feel herself slowly slipping back into a person she'd left behind in college, the old Katie Donovan, who relished walking around in bare feet—the Katie who turned to mush every time Grant Waverly smiled at her?

She knew she was a fool. No one had to point that out to her. But until she could honestly say Grant Waverly was entirely out of her system, she could not, in all good conscience, stay engaged to Charles. "I'm sorry, Charles. I'll see you when I get back. Until then, please consider our wedding called off.''

"Katie, I demand an explanation.''

"As soon as I find an explanation to give myself, you'll be the next to know. Goodbye, Charles.'' She hung up the phone and stood motionless, her hand resting on the receiver for a long time. The sparkle of her engagement ring caught her attention. Carefully, she slipped it from her finger and tucked it into the pocket of her robe.

Had she just thrown her future away for an insubstantial dream that had already blown up in her face once before? Had she just thrown away a man who would take care of her, love her, provide for her, and put her before anything else in his life—for a man who valued material possessions over love? Had she just admitted, in some obscure way, that there was a good chance she still loved Grant Waverly?

Chapter Seven

The following morning, an empty room bathed in sunlight bright enough to blind him greeted a sleepy-eyed Grant. As if that weren't enough, when he came down for breakfast, Harriet had reverted to her talkative self.

"Grant, dear. Good morning." She watched him slip into the chair at the breakfast table, then pour himself a cup of steaming fragrant coffee. "Oh my, you don't look good. Are you feeling all right, dear? Sometimes this change in climate can have—" She placed her hand over her mouth.

While he gave his answer some thought, Grant smiled halfheartedly over the rim of his cup at her knowing expression. He wasn't about to tell her he'd lain awake most of the night after Katie had come back to the room, not because of a night of passion, but because he'd been trying to figure out what was happening between them. That kind of confession would make its way back to Alfred and the board. He opted for ambiguous and to let her believe whatever she wanted.

"I'm fine. I just didn't get much sleep last night."

A dawning expression, followed by a blush washed over her face. "Of course you didn't. I told you that room brings out the romantic in people." She grinned at him, then busied herself whipping a bowl of batter. "Why, when my Alfred gets in there, he turns into a regular love savage...I hope everyone likes pancakes...they're my specialty...Alfred would be very put out if I didn't make them the first morning here." She added a large handful of what looked like tuna fish to the batter and began mixing again. "How many would you like, dear?"

While trying to imagine his boss playing the part of a love savage, he glanced at the lumpy mixture in the bowl. "I think I'll skip breakfast. Not very hungry. I'll have my coffee outside." With his stomach doing an imitation of a small boat riding out a hurricane, he slid from the chair.

Opening the door, he found himself wishing he'd stayed in the house and braved Harriet's specialty pancakes.

Katie occupied a deck chair close to the railing. Her sneakered feet rested on the rail. Long, tanned legs stretched out in front of her, ankles crossed. Her Florida tan glowed against her snowy shorts and Kelly-green blouse. She glanced at him, and the dark rings beneath her eyes told him he wasn't the only one who hadn't gotten a good night's sleep.

"Morning," she mumbled in his general direction.

"Morning." He wandered to the rail and gazed out toward Little Windsor and the open ocean.

A light fog, thinner than the one they'd come through the day before, but no less treacherous, lay over the water. In the distance, the blast of the foghorn took turns with the clang of the buoy marking the shoal between the big island and Little Windsor. Below them, the crash of heavy waves against the rocks throbbed like the heart of a giant beast.

"Harriet's packing a picnic lunch for us to take to Little Windsor today. I don't feel much like an outing. Could you make some excuse not to go?" Katie's voice sounded flat, and she didn't look at him, but instead fastened her gaze somewhere beyond the distant horizon.

What had her looking so grim? Was it the kiss they'd shared the evening before? And they *had* shared it. Of that Grant had no doubt.

Or did it have something to do with the trip she'd made downstairs after they'd all retired? Or was it just being with him? The thought made his stomach churn harder.

He understood Katie's reluctance, but felt it would probably be good for both of them to get their minds off things. "I think we should go. They'll be expecting us to have a good time while we're here, and Harriet is going to all the trouble to pack us lunch."

She glanced in his direction. "Did you check out those pancakes she's making? I came out here when she got out the can of tuna." An impish grin played around Katie's lush mouth, bringing a glint of life to her green eyes.

"Sure did. Why do you think I'm skipping breakfast?"

"Me, too." She brushed at a bright red curl the slight breeze had deposited across her cheek.

Grant caught a glimpse of her bare, left hand. *The engagement ring was gone.* He bit his tongue to keep from asking her where it was, what did its absence mean? Instead, he boosted himself onto the railing, fought back his elation, then doubled his efforts to persuade her to go.

"Why don't we take advantage of the getaway to the island? It might do us both good, release the tension of having to put up a front."

"I can't argue that. My nerves have about had it." Her tone had relaxed a bit already. Was she considering his suggestion?

He felt a surge of hope. Spending the day alone with Katie would be a trial, but spending it away from her would be even worse. "Then you'll go?"

She turned to look at him for the first time. She nodded, never taking her gaze from his. "I guess so." An unspoken question remained in her eyes.

"Don't worry. I'll behave."

She stared at him for a long time, then shrugged her shoulders, as if coming to some conclusion in her mind. A slow smile crept across her lips. "Did I ask you to behave?" She kicked off her sneakers, wiggled her bare toes against the wooden decking, then stood. "Let's see if Harriet has that picnic packed yet."

His heart somersaulted. *His* Katie was back. No telling what could happen today.

SHOES OFF, arms spread in abandonment, hair flying in the stiff ocean breeze, Katie stepped from the small boat Elmer had given them and picked her way over the uneven rocks comprising the jagged shoreline of Little Windsor. She sniffed the salt air to identify a vaguely familiar scent.

"Grant, there are wild strawberries here. We have to find them. I wonder if Harriet put anything in the basket that we can use to gather berries?" She tore her gaze from the ocean vista and turned to Grant. "Wild strawberries are sooo good." She licked her lips in anticipation of the treat she hadn't had since she'd visited her grandmother's farm in upstate New York at age five.

Grant had dragged the boat onto the rocks, then tied it to a scrubby, spruce tree. Now, he watched her, his hands on his hips and a wide smile curving his mouth.

Katie stared back. "What?"

He shook his head. "I am just enjoying the emergence of the old Katie. It's like watching a butterfly leave its cocoon."

The soft sound of his deep voice joined the salt spray washing over her from the waves hitting the slick rocks. For a long moment, their gazes held, and her mind ran to places she'd rather it didn't go.

Why had she agreed to this?

No need to ask that question twice. Back on the deck, she'd made up her mind to see where this thing with Grant would go. Heck, she'd made up her mind to that the night before, first with the kiss and then she'd verified it when she'd called off her wedding to Charles and removed her ring. But now that she stood face-to-face with the reality of her choices, doubts crept in. Was she opening herself up to more heartache?

Well, at this point, it seemed a little late to worry about that. She was already here and as far as heartache went, she knew how much it hurt to walk away from Grant. The question now seemed to be, was she willing to risk it again? Had she made a terrible mistake last night by breaking her engagement to Charles?

From the recesses of her mind came her mother's warning. *Marrying the wrong person for the wrong reasons can be as painful as losing the one you truly love.* But did she still love Grant?

More to the immediate point, after her coy little act on the deck, could she carry through on her suggestive remark, should the occasion arise? And if that familiar devilish gleam in his dark eyes meant what she thought it did, it had definite possibilities.

Before she could find answers, a noise, sounding much like a muffled dog's bark, came from the other side of the scrubby spruce.

She catapulted into Grant's arms. "What was that?"

He laughed and squeezed her. Looking down at her, he gently kissed her forehead. "It's just a gray seal. Remember, Harriet told us about them sunning themselves out here. Guess we disturbed him."

"A seal?" Katie looked over his shoulder in the

direction of a splash. In the water, just beyond the ragged ledge of rocks, she could see a dark, silky head and two very large, onyx eyes peering at her. Didn't she feel the fool? "Guess my nerves are still pretty frayed."

"You never were much of a nature girl." Grant tightened his hold on her. "And for the record—" he kissed her nose "—I'm not at all sorry you chose my arms for shelter."

Gazing up at him, she read desire in his darkening eyes. An answering flame flared to life inside her. *You know where this is going, Katie Maureen.* Ignoring her conscience's prodding, she continued to gaze into Grant's eyes.

"Katie, unless you're willing to take this to the next plateau, you better put some space between us—now." Strain colored his tone. Lines of tension etched themselves across his face. One dark eyebrow raised in a dare.

Katie detached herself from his embrace and moved several steps away. "Can I carry anything?" She pointed to the small pile of things Grant had taken from the boat.

Sighing and sucking in his breath for stability, Grant shook his head. "No. I can manage, as long as you don't tell me you want it on the other end of the island."

She looked at him cautiously, then seeing the playful expression he'd glued to his face for her benefit, grinned. "Let's leave it here until we decide where we'll be eating."

Like a woodland nymph in her bare feet, she darted off down the remnant of a path winding between overgrown banks of wild, pink-to-white island roses. Their blooms danced as she brushed past. The heady perfume of some late-blooming lilacs filled the warm air. In the background, the Seal Point Lighthouse waited for darkness to shine its one-eyed beacon over the dark waters of the Atlantic. He smiled. It was going to be one hell of a day. Even Mother Nature was cooperating.

Grant delved into the hamper, found two sandwiches in plastic bags, removed them, stuffed the bags in his shorts pocket, then closed the hamper. Leaving behind the picnic hamper, the towels and the two thin, flannel blankets encased in a plastic bag Harriet had provided to keep them dry, he trudged after Katie.

By the time he rounded a corner in the path, Katie had pried loose a board from a missing window, and was peeking inside the deserted cottage they'd spotted on their way to the island. Squeezing herself through the opening, she disappeared inside the cottage. He followed her.

"Isn't this exciting, Grant? Who do you suppose lived here? Maybe a whole family."

Grant glanced around the small house. Musty and dark, but in amazingly good repair, it contained little furniture—a table and three chairs. The one large room boasted a fireplace on one side next to a window that overlooked Penobscot Bay and two windows overlooking the open ocean on the other—all boarded up except the one they'd entered through. A dinner-plate-size hole in the roof near the front eave provided a light source for them to explore by.

"I doubt it. Place doesn't look big enough for more than two people." He pointed at the hole in the roof. "Great air-conditioning system, though."

Busy digging under the pile of firewood stacked neatly beside the hearth, Katie either didn't hear him or was ignoring him. She picked something up. "Look at this." She extended a small piece of plastic to him. "It looks like the end of a baby's rattle."

He took it and rubbed at the dirt still clinging to it with the pad of his thumb. Katie was right. The twisted pink plastic had definitely been attached to a baby rattle at one time. "A girl, if the color means anything." He handed it back to her.

"Of course it means something. Color with babies is very important. If they're born bald as a billiard ball, it's difficult to tell the sex just by looking at them." She caressed the plastic, then laid it carefully on the corner of the hearth. "Wonder where that little girl is now."

Stopping in his study of a piece of rock streaked with gray and green that made up part of the fireplace, Grant saw the opening he'd been waiting for and went to stand beside Katie. "I never knew you were so fond of kids."

"I want a houseful."

"*You* want a houseful. What about what's-his-name?"

She moved away and looked out the window that

faced the big island. "Is this where you try to convince me you didn't notice my engagement ring is off my finger?"

"No. I noticed, but I'm not sure what it means." He held his breath.

"It means the wedding is off."

Silence strung out between them, while Grant tried to assess her reaction to this.

He wanted to ask her if she loved Charles. If she had ever loved him. But he didn't ask. Believing that she didn't love Charles and never had, that she'd broken the engagement because of Grant and not anything that had to do with Charles was easier. Grant didn't stop to analyze why that was so important to a man who had no intention of getting involved, especially with a woman who didn't understand his goals in life.

"I'm sorry." Grant didn't know anything else safe to say. He couldn't trust himself to say more. The elation he'd experienced back at The Homeplace, when he'd first noticed her bare finger, spread through him, drowning out reason and intelligent thought.

Katie turned to gaze at him. Her eyes full of emotion. "Are you really sorry?"

"No." His reply hung in a silence ripe with suggestion.

KATIE PICKED SEVERAL red berries and dropped them in the plastic bag she held. Her gaze wandered first to a scattering of clouds overhead, then to Grant sitting on a rock near the ocean's edge. Things were happening between them, things she wasn't sure she wanted to happen. At the same time, she felt powerless to prevent them and eager to embrace them.

Grant had noticed her missing ring and knew that Charles no longer stood between them. Would he take advantage of the new set of circumstances? Did she want him to?

"Hey! No daydreaming. You're supposed to be gathering enough of those things for desert." Grant had come to stand beside her.

"I was looking at the ocean," she lied. "It's so strong, so determined. It seems to know exactly where it's going and won't let anything stand in its way." She glanced at his strong profile. "Reminds me of you, and your one-sided quest for a career."

Placing his index finger under her chin, Grant raised her face. She stared into his dark, mesmerizing eyes. "We're not going there today. Every time we do, it causes trouble. I want today to be special." He waited. "Okay?"

She nodded then stepped away from him, unable to control the sensations his nearness evoked.

He seemed genuinely glad she'd let the subject of his career drop. Odd. She could never recall a time during college when Grant hadn't been eager to discuss his legal career with anyone and everyone. Now, he was going out of his way to avoid it. Very odd.

"What's this?" she asked, picking up his plastic bag from where he'd placed it on the rocks bordering the strawberry patch. Inside the bag rested colored chunks of something he'd been gathering while she picked strawberries. "Looks like glass to me." She slung the bag against his chest and grinned.

Catching the bag, he answered her grin with one of his own. "It is glass. Sea glass. Regular glass worn smooth by the ocean. Harriet collects it, and I thought I'd take some back for her."

"Admirable, but we can't eat glass, Waverly. Get busy picking."

"I assumed, since you're the expert on wild berries, that you'd make sure there were enough for both of us."

She stepped back and smiled, waving the bag of luscious red berries at him. "Sorry. Them what don't pick, don't eat."

"Oh, no?" He tucked his bag of sea glass into his pocket and started toward her, a gleam of devilishness lighting his eyes. "Didn't your mother ever teach you to share?"

"Didn't yours ever teach you that little boys who take things from little girls are bullies?" She backed up farther.

He followed her, the gleam never leaving his eyes. "My mother taught me to take what I wanted." His gaze traveled up her tanned legs to her face. "And in case your mirror's been lying to you, Miss Donovan, you are no longer a little girl."

His gazed burned through her clothing to her sensitive skin. Katie's senses came to full alert. It was too soon. She hadn't had time to think this out yet. In defense, she continued the game. "Gotta catch me first," she called over her shoulder, taking off at a dead run toward the cottage.

Hot on her heels, Grant pursued her. She ducked around in front of the cottage, then made for the lighthouse. Grant followed. Her laughter spilled out over the rocks as she darted around the lighthouse and headed back toward the cottage. She stepped around the corner of the building and straight into Grant's arms. Laughing, they tumbled breathlessly to the ground in a tangle of arms and legs.

He pinned her beneath him, their faces inches apart. "Are you going to share or do I have to take what's mine?" His chest expanded against her sensitive breasts.

Suddenly, the laughter went out of both of them. The atmosphere tingled with emotion. Sensations of erotic pleasure raced up and down Katie's body. It had been a long time since she'd been this close to Grant. Amazingly, her body hadn't forgotten. In fact, it responded stronger now than she ever recalled before.

The suddenness of her body's response frightened her. She squirmed from beneath him and held out the plastic bag she'd still clutched in her hand. "Here. Take them."

Grant sat back on his haunches. "We both know I wasn't asking about strawberries, Katie." He stood, ran his hands through his hair and gazed out to sea. "Have I been reading you wrong since I met you on the deck this morning?"

She couldn't look at him. He hadn't been reading

her wrong. She'd been throwing out signals all day. And now that he seemed prepared to take her up on her offers, the consequences of what she wanted to do were preventing her from making the move.

"Give me some time, Grant. This is a big step for me."

He stared at her for a long moment, then nodded. "Okay. We'll play this your way." He extended his hand to her. "Come on, let's go get the picnic hamper and have lunch."

She took his hand and squeezed it. "Thanks."

"For what?"

"Understanding."

He laughed aloud. "Katie, any man who claims to understand you is in big trouble."

She glared at him, grinned, then punched his arm.

As they walked silently back to the boat to gather the things they'd left behind, Grant stole glances at Katie's profile. What had stopped her? He'd read the desire in her eyes. She'd wanted to continue as badly as he had. Why had she stopped him? Was it because of Charles? Did she really love him?

No. He'd have staked his life on the fact that Katie might be very fond of her ex-fiancé, but love had never entered the picture. At least, from her side, it hadn't. He recalled when he'd first told her about them being married. Katie's first concern should have been that the situation would, in some way, keep her from the man she loved. Instead, she'd been concerned more about a cake with no one to eat it than she had about Charles.

No. Charles wasn't the problem here. At least Grant didn't think he was. Maybe, she—

Two very large drops of rain hit his face, stirring him from his troubling thoughts.

"Grant, it's raining. The lunch!"

They ran toward the boat, but the rain increased almost instantly to a downpour, soaking them and everything around them in seconds. When they reached the hamper, he opened it to find soggy sandwiches lying atop soggy cake. Thanks goodness Harriet had put the towels and blankets in a plastic bag.

A sudden, strong wind caught the top and blew the basket over, spilling its contents on the rocks. Quickly, Grant scooped up the spilled food and then shoved it back in the basket.

Keeping his foot on the basket so it wouldn't blow away, he thrust the plastic bag of linens into Katie's arms. "Take these. I'll grab the picnic hamper. We'll take shelter in the cottage till this blows over, then head back to The Homeplace."

FIFTEEN MINUTES LATER, while Grant coaxed a fire to life in the fireplace, Katie sorted through the soggy contents of the picnic hamper. Outside, driven by a stiff northeastern wind off the ocean, the rain pounded against the roof and the walls. In the far corner of the building, a puddle grew beneath the hole in the roof, but where she and Grant were remained snug and dry.

Katie stood beside the table, which she'd covered with the bright-blue plastic tablecloth Harriet had tucked into the bottom of the hamper. Slowly, she sifted through the soggy remnants of their proposed lunch.

Near her, on his knees on the floor, Grant blew into the struggling flame on the damp dried grass they'd managed to gather from beneath the eaves of the house. The flame caught and soon the sound of a crackling fire filled the air, along with the pungent scent of burning driftwood. He kept a close eye on the fire's progress as he spread one of the blankets before the hearth.

"So much for lunch," Katie announced, holding out for Grant's inspection a soggy white glob that had once been a chicken salad sandwich.

He curled his nose. "Is it all ruined?"

"No." She grinned and dug into the basket. "There's cheese and a thermos of coffee and…this." She brandished a bottle of champagne and two crystal goblets in the growing firelight.

A chuckle escaped Grant. He shook his head. "You really gotta give Harriet points for trying."

Katie frowned. His words puzzled her. She thought Harriet had done an admirable job on the picnic. "Trying?"

"To patch up our troubled marriage. She obviously thought out the contents of that basket quite thoroughly before she packed it. Everything we'd need to set the right atmosphere for the day." Through the window from which they'd removed the boards, he pointed at the boiling clouds and the sheets of water descending on them from the heavens. "Knowing her, she probably ordered this storm."

Busily assessing the beginning of his statement about the romantic atmosphere, Katie barely heard his last words. She looked around her. A deserted cottage, an isolated island, a bottle of champagne and the one man in the world who could turn her into a wanton just by smiling at her. Oh, heavens, she was in very big trouble.

She sneezed. *Great!* On top of everything else, she'd probably end up with pneumonia from these wet clothes. She plucked at the material clinging to her skin.

"We'd better get you out of your clothes."

"What?" Katie stared at Grant.

He shook his head. "Don't worry. I'm not going to turn into a dirty old man. I'm just thinking about you catching cold." He stood.

Frantically, her gaze darted around the room, seeking out a place where she could possibly do what he had suggested. Nothing. Only open space.

"I'll hold up a blanket and you can change behind it."

"Into what?" Even she could hear the near panic tinting her voice.

"Wrap yourself in the other blanket. I'm sure there's enough material there to more than adequately preserve your modesty." Bending, he picked up the blanket and, grabbing two corners, held the blanket at arm's length above his head, forming a dressing room of sorts beside the blazing fire. He waited.

Could she do this? Knowing how close she was to

throwing herself in his arms, could she spend the next few hours alone with him in this cottage—naked?

She sneezed again.

"Bless you. Now stop being stubborn and get those clothes off."

Seeing no other alternative, Katie slowly peeled her drenched clothes from her body. All the time, she kept a sharp eye on the blanket for any sign that he might decide to drop it. Once the clothes were gone, she grabbed the extra blanket and wrapped it around her shoulders, clutching it closed from the inside.

"I'm done." A large drop of rainwater rolled out of her hairline and down her forehead. She swiped at it with the corner of the blanket.

Grant dropped the blanket and stared at her for a moment. "Come here and I'll dry your hair." He put down the blanket and shook out a towel from the pile she'd placed on the table.

"I can do my own hair."

"Oh? And exactly how do you plan on keeping that blanket around you while you accomplish this?" He arched one black eyebrow and continued to stare at her.

She eyed him with an I'll-show-you expression, then, after straightening the blanket he'd dropped to the floor, she kneeled on it, facing the fire. Taking the towel from him, she leaned forward. The blanket hung around her shoulders to form an open-front tent. She threw the towel over her head, then began to rub at her wet hair.

She couldn't see Grant, but she could feel him

moving about the room. The fire on her naked skin warmed her flesh in seconds. Already, she felt better.

Suddenly, the towel was removed from her fingers. Out of the corner of her eye, she could see Grant standing beside her wrapped in one of the towels she'd left on the table. Her gaze traveled up his strong legs to his ribbed stomach and lightly haired chest, then to his face.

"You're kneeling on the other blanket, sweet," he murmured in answer to her unspoken question.

Without another word, he began to rub her hair, his fingers plowing through the curls, skimming over her suddenly overly sensitive scalp. The pressure of his ministrations bent her head forward. She had an unobstructed view of her own bare breasts. The nipples had hardened into two pebbles of desire. Quickly, she hauled the blanket around her, then struggled to her feet.

Carefully skirting him, she began pulling what was left of their lunch from the hamper and laying it out on one of the china plates Harriet had packed. "We'd better get something to eat. If the storm stops, we'll be able to go back to the island and—"

Grant raised her face to his with a finger under her chin. "Running again, Katie M.?"

Keeping her gaze on her task, she laughed nervously. "How can I run? Where is there to run to? I was just—"

Again, he stopped her words with a finger, this time to her lips. It felt warm and the sensations his touch to her sensitive mouth evoked oozed over her, swamping her thoughts. "Running," he said. His voice mesmerized her.

Taking the food from her hands, he laid it back on the table, then led her to the blanket. Holding her shoulders, he eased her down. Katie's heart pounded. Her breath came in uneven drafts of craved air. She closed her eyes, waiting. Waiting.

Nothing happened. She opened them and found him sitting across from her, the towel tucked neatly between his thighs. In his hand, he held the bottle of champagne. He twisted off the wire, then popped the cork and filled the two goblets. In each, he floated one of the wild strawberries. He handed her one of the glasses.

She gazed at him trancelike, while he retrieved the berry from his glass and then bit it in half. When he discarded the remainder, she roused herself from her sensual stupor to stop him.

"Wait. You're wasting half the berry. Let me show you." She tucked the blanket under her armpits, to free her hands. Then she selected a fat berry from the sandwich bag and dropped it in her glass. "Eating strawberries in champagne is an art. Watch."

Capturing the plump berry by the cap of green leaves, she slid the fruit between her lips, sipping at the champagne clinging to the outside. Satisfied that no more champagne remained, she bit into the berry and pulled the cap off, leaving none of the luscious fruit to go to waste.

"Understand?" she asked, smiling at him.

Grant understood all right. He understood he'd just

witnessed one of the most erotic sights he'd ever been fortunate enough to observe. He understood that the blanket hovered a hairsbreadth from revealing more than her creamy shoulders. He understood that his libido had jumped close to the loss-of-control level. He understood they were playing with fire and he didn't give a damn.

Katie handed him a berry. "Now you do it."

He sipped from his glass, eyeing her over the rim. Placing his goblet on the floor, he plucked the strawberry from the champagne. Holding her prisoner with his eyes, he carefully laved the champagne from the berry, just as she'd done, but he added his own touch. Curling his tongue around the fruit, he passed it between his lips, sucking gently on it. With a hint of a smile, he released it from his lips and then leaned toward her. Using the berry, he outlined her mouth, letting her taste him on its shining skin. He slid it between her open lips.

"Bite," he commanded softly, his face inches from hers.

Doing as she was told, Grant held her gaze with his. As her teeth punctured the succulent, tender flesh of the fruit, the juice exploded and a drop trickled from the corner of her mouth. Grant caught it with his thumb, then pushing his finger between her lips, he rubbed it over the tender skin on the inside of her bottom lip. With the innocence of a child, as he withdrew his thumb from her mouth, she instinctively sucked the last drop from his thumb. The heady aroma of strawberries filled the room, blending with the scent of burning wood.

He pressed the remainder of the berry to her lips. She bit down. Grant quickly captured the juice escaping her mouth with his tongue. Savoring the taste of her skin, he deftly removed each drop of ruby juice. As before, he returned it to her, this time swirling his tongue over the inside of her mouth, tasting her sweetness mixing with the strawberry's acidity. When he had satisfied himself with her inner flavors, he licked the juice from her lips, then laved up the few drops that had landed on her chest.

Katie groaned and writhed against him.

He'd been wrong. This was not the old Katie. This woman responding to his every caress held more fire and passion than the youthful girl he'd loved seven years ago. For a moment, he experienced a razor-sharp pang of regret at having missed those years in between and watching her become a woman. Then he became lost in the woman bathed in firelight and shadows.

Chapter Eight

That her champagne goblet had slipped from her nerveless fingers barely penetrated Katie's sensual state. Her mind, this little cottage, the world outside had blended into one thing—Grant and his arousing touch. Gently, he eased her back to lie full-length on the blanket spread before the fire in the island cottage.

Never disturbing the thin flannel covering her, Grant smoothed his hand over her breasts and stomach, caressing her skin with the soft material. Her insides quivered. When he reached her stomach, he pulled the blanket taut. Her nipples hardened in response to the friction of the flannel sliding over them.

Katie moaned and twisted to escape the sensual pleasure of his touch, but she remained his willing captive, trapped by her growing desires. Experiencing demands and needs she hadn't felt since the last time with Grant, she surrendered herself to his relentless tenderness.

The urgency of riding atop a runaway team of horses heading toward a sheer cliff invaded Grant. But he held back. Selfishly, he wanted the plunge over the precipice to be the most cataclysmic of Katie's life—something she'd *never* forget. Pleased with the rapid beat of her heart and the soft, jerky drafts of strawberry-scented breath coming from her parted lips, he repeated the stroking.

Gathering a wad of material in his fingers, he slid his hand to the juncture of her thighs. He slipped his foot beneath the blanket, then hooked her leg, drawing it to him, gently separating her thighs. With the ball of fabric, he rubbed in slow, tantalizing circles over the highly sensitized flesh between her legs.

A cry of intense pleasure broke from her. Her nails dug into his shoulders. Her back arched, pressing her breasts against his naked chest. The blanket slithered to her waist. His towel slipped away.

Keeping the thin blanket sandwiched between them, he covered her with his body, sliding his thigh between her legs, fueling the flames ignited by his hand. The cool material quickly absorbed the heat of their flesh, becoming a slippery, hot conductor of erotic sensations.

"Do...you...feel...it, too?" she gasped.

"Yes, my Katie." He outlined the flower of her ear with kisses. "I feel it in every pulse of your blood, every quiver of your body, every rasp of your breath. It's burning through me like a hot poker."

The words had stolen what little breath his laboring lungs permitted him. His body throbbed with the need to fully possess her as he moved his leg and slid his hand to the nub of her desire.

"Please, stay with me."

Grant knew, deep inside, she meant only for this moment. "I will. With every beat of your heart." He moaned with the pain of passion and with the certainty that, when this was all over, Katie might walk away, and he would be powerless to stop her. He banished all such thoughts from his mind and concentrated on the warm woman clinging to him.

As the speed of his massaging hand increased, so did Katie's need. She spiraled toward an end that waited tantalizingly just beyond reach. She strained toward it, knowing if she didn't reach it, she'd die from her aching need. Grant's hand movements intensified. She felt his probing finger enter her. The world spun out of control and slowly restored itself to orbit.

When she opened her eyes, Grant looked down at her with an expression she had never seen on a man's face before. He adored her with his eyes. Love swelled inside her. Robbed of controlled breath, she slid her arms around his neck, questioning him with her eyes.

"Next time, you'll touch the stars," he told her. He lowered his mouth to hers. He parted her lips and explored the inside of her mouth.

The breathlessness started again, building, driving her toward another out-of-control journey to the stars. Delicious pressure built inside her, surprising her with its sudden surge. She felt Grant pull back and protested with her clinging hands.

"My Katie," he soothed, kicking the blanket aside. "This time we'll fly with the angels." He lowered his head and sampled a swollen nipple, drawing the extended nub into his mouth, suckling with all the greed of a child at his mother's breast.

Though his desire grew with each touch, each kiss, he held back. This *must* be the greatest experience of Katie's life. He wouldn't settle for less, even if it meant he had to endure the tortures of hell.

"Please." The plea left her lips on an erratic gust of air. She arched against him, twisting and turning, reaching for the heavens.

Spurred on by Katie's plea, Grant's emotions hurtled out of control. He positioned himself over her and held her close.

"Help me love you, my Katie." He entered the haven of her body and surrendered himself to sensation.

She stared up at him. The firm set of his mouth, the hungry flames in his eyes, told her he'd join her in her breathless flight into the exploding heavens. Together they touched the stars and soared out into the universe. Colored lights burst inside her head, blinking on and off, and rushing over her in waves of throbbing brilliance. A new life seeped into her— Grant. At that moment, she knew part of her would belong to him—forever.

GRANT LAY VERY STILL, fighting for his breath and coherent thought. He'd never experienced such a raw need since his last time with Katie. Her silky body beneath him. Her arms and legs holding him close. The rapture of being encased in her heat. He felt as though he'd absorbed her into his soul. At last, he had his Katie back.

Perfect. Everything was perfect.

He glanced at Katie curled in his arms, the firelight dancing over her skin. She looked so peaceful, so lovely. Perhaps now they could make a life together. She still cared about him. No woman could respond like she did to his lovemaking and not care. And she had to realize that he loved her, had never stopped.

Once he moved her to Miami and they got married, this obsession she had about his job being more important than she was would soon be put to rest. If it hadn't already. He and Katie were finally on the road to happiness.

"Grant?"

"Hmm?" He kissed her hair, then stroked her flushed cheek with the pad of his thumb.

"Shouldn't we be getting back soon? Alfred and Harriet will worry."

He raised on one elbow to look out the window at the darkening sky. "I'm afraid we aren't going anywhere for a while."

Katie struggled up to sit beside him, then cocked her head, listening for the rain that had poured down on the little cottage for hours. "Why? I don't hear anything."

"You don't hear fog, sweet."

"Fog?" She swung away from him and looked out at the wall of white mist beyond the window.

"It would be sheer stupidity for me to try to find my way past the shoal to the big island in this." He noted that the blanket had slipped to Katie's waist, baring her breasts to the firelight. "Guess we'll just have to stay here and find something less dangerous to keep us occupied till morning." He ran a fingertip around the dark aureole of one breast.

Katie grinned and turned back to face him. "I thought you said *less* dangerous."

He kissed her hard. "There's dangerous, then there's *dangerous*," he growled against her eager mouth. Pressing her back to the floor, he covered her body with his.

THE SUN SHONE brightly on the small island when Katie and Grant opened their eyes the next morning. Katie stretched her well-used muscles and looked up at the man studying her from above. She wanted to throw herself in his arms. But she'd awakened with old ghosts taunting her.

"Do you suppose we'll ever come to any agreement about our differences?"

"I thought we did that last night."

Katie sat up, hauling the blanket with her. She wrapped her nudity in flannel, safe from his eyes. "No. We didn't. What we did was make love, something we've never had a problem with, even seven years ago."

"Then I'm afraid I don't see the problem." He reached for her, but she slid backward, just beyond his fingertips.

He's evading the issue. She wanted this out in the open and settled. They had no future if it wasn't.

"That's the trouble. You never did see a problem." A sudden sadness cloaked his features. "The problem is the same one that never seems to go away completely. What do we do about us?"

He stared at her for a long moment. She always loved the way Grant looked after making love, rumpled and cuddly.

"Is there an *us,* Katie?"

"That's up to you." She waited for his reply. So much hinged on his answer.

"Once I get this promotion, there's nothing stopping us."

"If we love each other, why should our happiness depend on your career?"

"Why can't we have both?" His gaze pleaded for her to agree, but she couldn't do it.

"Because your drive to further your career will eventually kill our love. There will always be another promotion, always another step on the ladder to scale. Your job will always come between us. Eventually, it'll sap all your time and energies. So much so that there won't be anything left for us." She prayed for him to understand, to not throw away what they could have again.

Grant wanted to argue that point, but he still had a vivid memory of the past two years without a social life and without the time to spend more than a few hours in his apartment. And there was also the senior partnership. How could she ask him to trash his dreams? Together, they could make this work.

Apart... "With you in Miami, it won't be that bad. We'll have plenty of time together."

"Miami? Why would I want to be in Miami?"

"I thought that, when we get back, you could move down there so we'd be able to start our life together." If just this once he could make her see reason, perhaps they could get past this wall that seemed to grow like an unwanted weed between them.

"Are you forgetting I already have a life in St. Augustine, a business, a home of my own, my family?"

"You can start a new business in Miami. People all over want antiques."

"That's not the point. I have a life, and you want me to throw it all away on the off chance that we might be able to make this relationship work. That's a pretty big gamble, considering that I'm the one making all the concessions."

"You are?" Grant saw red. "What about my life, my dreams? Aren't you asking me to do the same thing? It seems to me that I'm taking some pretty big chances here, too. There's a good chance I can make senior partner, if I stay with Alfred. Do you have any idea what that could mean to us?"

"You just don't get it, do you?" Katie stared at him, then shook her head. "Why do we keep beating this dead horse? We couldn't agree on this seven years ago and we certainly aren't any closer to agreement now." She sighed, admitting defeat. "We should just finish out this little drama we're enacting for Harriet and Alfred, then go back to our separate lives. Once the annulment comes through, we'll both be free to go our own way.''

''But—''

She held up her hand. ''No more, Grant. Please, no more. We go in huge circles and always end up at the same impasse.''

Katie stood, trying not to fall on her face by getting her feet tangled in the blanket's folds. She walked slowly to the chair where she'd hung her clothes to dry before the hearth. ''I'd appreciate it if you'd hold the blanket, so I can dress.''

Odd request coming from a woman who'd just shared the most intimate of acts with the same man she now wanted to hide her nudity from. But then, hiding would also cover the tears running freely down her cheeks and the broken heart spilling from her chest. Or at least, that's how it felt.

She felt trapped. Trapped in a situation of her own making. Why had she ever thought that making love with Grant would change him, would change her, would change what they both wanted from life?

When they walked out of this cottage, she would still want children and a husband who loved them all more than everything else in his life—the kind of love her father had been unable to give her mother and her. A life with Grant would take on all the aspects of what she'd endured throughout her childhood. She couldn't face that kind of loneliness and she wouldn't ask a child to face it.

Feeling like a fraud, she stood on the other side of

the blanket Grant held high, absorbing his nearness to store away for the time when he would be gone.

When she'd finished dressing, she stepped from behind the blanket. "Please get dressed and take me back to The Homeplace. I'll wait for you in the boat."

She walked from the cottage without looking back. She didn't trust herself. Because, if she hadn't learned anything else in the past few hours with Grant, she'd managed to get one thing very clear in her mind. She could very easily learn to love Grant Waverly all over again—if she hadn't already.

"THANK GOODNESS, they're back," Harriet announced to Alfred. "I watched from the upstairs window till they docked the boat." She hurried past him to the living room window overlooking the front of the house.

When Grant and Katie hadn't returned the day before, she'd been terrified, but both Alfred and Elmer had managed to calm her some with the assurance that the cottage would offer the couple shelter until the storm blew itself out. However, when the fog rolled in as thick as cotton candy, she'd begun to pace all over again. It had taken Alfred hours to convince her that Grant was smart enough to stay put until he could find his way back to Windsor Island in the daylight.

"Now, Harriet, don't fawn over them. They're adults and they don't need you mothering them." Alfred folded his newspaper, laid it on the family room sofa, then stood and joined her at the window. Over her shoulder, he watched with her as Grant made his way up the hill alone.

She craned her neck, her gaze scanning the trees to either side of Grant. "Where's Katie?"

"Over there, on the lawn, next to the rose garden." Alfred pointed over her shoulder.

Pushing aside the drape, she could see Katie sitting on the lawn near the rose garden, her back to the house, her head resting on her bent legs. Her shoulders moved.

"Why the poor child is crying." Harriet turned toward the front door, but before she could take a step, Alfred snagged her arm.

"Leave her alone. They've obviously had a quarrel and the last thing she needs is the embarrassment of your discovering her."

"But—"

"Harriet." Alfred leveled her objection with a stern gaze he usually reserved for Raymond back at the office when the boy left his endless trail of cookie crumbs across the clean carpet. "You will *not* interfere."

The man could be so unreasonable when he wanted to be. Why couldn't she have married an amiable sort like herself? Obviously, the poor child needed someone to talk to. If not her, then who? If only Katie's mother were here, Harriet was sure she'd know what to do. *Her mother.* Of course. "If you won't let me talk to her, at least let me call her mother and bring her here to speak with Katie. At a time like this, a girl needs her mother's wisdom."

"Absolutely not." Pulling her away from the window, he sat Harriet in one of the leather wingback chairs near the fireplace. "Grant and Katie have the right to expect us to stay out of their affairs. I went along with your scheme to bring them here because I saw it as a way to help them over a rough spot in their marriage. But beyond that, we should leave it to them." He straightened and moved to the sofa, where he once more picked up his newspaper. "Stop meddling, Harriet. If Katie and Grant can't settle their differences, I'll just have to drop him from the list of junior partner candidates."

Harriet glared at her husband. "Candidates?" She sprang to her feet. "Candidates? Is that all you see in these two young people? A new junior partner and his charming wife?" Striding to Alfred's side, she yanked the newspaper from his hands and tore it neatly down the middle, then tore it again and dropped it on the floor.

"Harriet! What in blazes— Have you lost what little mind God gave you, woman?" Alfred's face bloomed a marvelous cherry red. At last she'd gotten his full attention.

"Do you ever think of anything beyond that blessed office? This is the happiness of two human beings, two human beings who love each other very much. Now, I don't know what you intend to do, but I'm going to do whatever I can to prevent them from making the worst mistake of their lives." She picked up the receiver on the phone at Alfred's elbow. "I'm calling Katie's mother and telling her her daughter needs her. What's her name?''

Alfred jerked the phone from her grasp and replaced the receiver. "You will not drag Elizabeth Donovan into this.''

Placing her nose within inches of his, Harriet gave a very unladylike snort. "I will.''

"You will not.''

She reached for the phone, but Alfred was quicker. He hid it behind his back. "I forbid it.'' His gaze blazed down at her. "Now find something else to keep you busy besides sticking your nose into other people's lives.''

In all their married years, Harriet had very seldom heard her husband take that tone with her or seen him look more adamant. The biggest share of the time, he yessed her to death to keep her silent. She'd lost the battle, but not the war.

"Very well, Alfred," she said in her iciest tone. "But I am going out there and see if I can do anything to help that poor child, whether you like it or not.'' As she rounded the doorway of the living room, she plucked her camera off a side table, then cast a try-and-stop-me look back at her husband.

Alfred threw a glare her way. She returned it in kind, then stomped from the room.

"Men!'' The divine powers-that-be should have devised a way for women to live without males. Especially when they got sassy.

"KATIE, DEAR. I'm so glad you and Grant made it back all right. Was the night on the island too bad?''

Katie knew that Harriet could see the traces of tears on her cheeks, even though she'd done her best to remove them and dry her eyes on her blouse sleeve.

"It wasn't bad." In fact it was one of the most wonderful nights of her life. The tears threatened again, but Katie fought them back.

Harriet's arm slid around Katie's shoulders. The camera hanging around Harriet's neck, banged against Katie's shoulder. "Then what's the trouble, dear?" She brushed at a stray drop of moisture on Katie's cheek and smiled. "Want to talk about it?"

Yes, she wanted to talk about it, but how could she tell Harriet that Grant wanted to ruin their lives before they even got started? "No. I'll be okay. Just a little married tiff."

"Hmm. Men are beasts, aren't they?" Harriet flopped down on the grass beside Katie. "Sometimes, I'd like to grab Alfred by the shirt collar and shake the tar out of him."

Katie glanced at Harriet. She wasn't just saying things to make Katie feel better. From the anger apparent in Harriet's expression, she and Alfred had obviously had a fight about something, too.

"But that's no reason to find solace elsewhere, my dear."

Baffled by Harriet's words, Katie stared at her. "I don't understand what you mean. Solace elsewhere?" Was Harriet contemplating an affair and trying to talk herself out of it?

"An affair…"

Harriet waited, it seemed to Katie, for her to fill in the blank. "An affair?"

"Oh dear, I've come this far, I might just as well spill it all." Harriet, wiggled her behind to a more comfortable position in the grass. Obviously, this was going to be a long confession.

"When you and Grant came to the country club that night, and you went to the ladies' room, I came to get you." Harriet paused and looked around, as if she might be overheard by some invisible eavesdropper. "I saw you kissing a gentleman outside before you got into his car." She grabbed Katie's hand. "I'm so sorry, dear. I didn't do it to spy. It just was…well, it was just there. That's when Alfred and I decided to bring you and Grant up here to mend your marriage."

Katie sat in stunned silence for a long moment.

Harriet saw me kissing Charles.

Suddenly, Katie began laughing. If this wasn't the capper to an otherwise horrible day, she didn't know what could be. Harriet and Alfred thought she was having an affair with her fiancé and had brought her and Grant here to patch up a marriage that never really existed.

Brow furrowed, Harriet looked on. "I'm afraid I don't get the joke, dear."

Katie stopped. She couldn't ruin Grant's chances by going into the real story. So how could she explain kissing Charles when Harriet believed she was married to Grant?

"That was my…brother. Yes. Charles is my brother. That's why I was kissing him…hadn't seen him for a few months…he just showed up out of nowhere. Imagine running into him at that very country club. Talk about your coincidences—"

She stopped herself. She was beginning to sound like Harriet. Katie's hostess wasn't the brightest woman Katie had ever encountered, but she certainly wasn't a complete fool.

"Oh. Your brother. Well, that certainly takes a load off my mind." Harriet paused. Her brow furrowed. "But it doesn't explain why you were crying."

Katie hugged her hostess briefly. "I was just a bit down. Rain does that to me."

For a long tense moment, Harriet stared back at Katie. "Very well. We'll have to see what we can do to cheer you up. Maybe some lawn games later, huh?"

Knowing it would take more than games to erase the depression that had settled over Katie on the island, she smiled.

Relief washed over Harriet's expression. It warmed Katie's heart that the woman had worried so much about the incident. But it also upset Katie that she and Grant were deceiving two very nice, caring people. Her mood took a plunge a little deeper into the well of despair.

"Well, now that we have that settled, I wonder if I could prevail on you to take some pictures of my prize roses. The rose show is next week and I have to get my entry in." Slipping her camera strap over her head, Harriet extended the small black rectangle to Katie.

Stunned, Katie stared it. It had more dials and settings than an airplane cockpit. "Me take pictures? I'm afraid I don't—"

"—don't take any when you're on vacation? I understand dear, and normally I would never impose on you...but I really would appreciate it if you'd make an exception this time...this rose competition means so much to me. That Myrtle Wentworth has won it five years in a row...oh, I don't mind her winning...it's just that she lords it over everyone for weeks...and one of these fine days, I may have to pop the old bag."

Before Harriet could get any more wound up, Katie took the camera from her. She had absolutely no idea what to do, but she figured if she turned enough dials and flicked enough settings, something would happen.

"I'm not sure this light is going to be right for the pictures to be at their best," she said, moving about the garden and peering through the viewfinder as if she knew what she was doing.

"Just do what you can, dear."

Before Katie started, she had to ask Harriet a question that burned in her mind since the day they'd first arrived here. "Harriet, does Alfred's work interfere with your private life?"

A shrill note of humor erupted from Harriet. "Oh, my. All the time, my dear, all the time. But one learns to live for the moments you do have together and make them special and apart from the rest. I do believe in many ways, the fact that I see so little of Alfred has strengthened our relationship." She cupped her hand around her mouth, as if afraid of being overheard. "I'm certain I would have done him bodily harm otherwise."

She sidestepped Katie and moved to the far side of the garden where a white rose held its pristine face to the sun. The petals looked like snow.

"This is my prize," Harriet announced proudly. She caressed a petal with her fingertip, as if stroking a baby's face.

Katie joined her. On one petal a small drop of moisture from their recent watering glistened in the sunlight. "The water on the petal looks like a diamond," she said, admiring silently the perfection of the flower.

"That's what I've called it. White Diamond." Harriet's chest swelled with pride. "I cultivated it myself over the past few years."

Probably had nothing else to do, Katie thought. What with Alfred at the office till all hours, what else could Harriet do but find a hobby to fill the time? That wasn't what Katie wanted. Why couldn't she make Grant see that? Why was she even trying?

After this vacation ended, she'd put Grant behind her, just as she'd done when she left college and returned home short of finishing her junior year. All it had taken was a little determination.

As Katie tried to find the perfect White Diamond in the viewfinder, she knew in her heart that this time determination wouldn't be nearly enough to forget Grant. This time she needed a miracle.

Chapter Nine

Grant wandered into the library, hoping to find a book that would bore him sufficiently to put him to sleep and help him forget that Katie slept not twelve feet away from him. Surprised to find the fireplace crackling away and Alfred ensconced in a wingback chair with a snifter of brandy in his hand, Grant cleared his throat to make his presence known.

Alfred glanced up from his deep contemplation of the jagged flames. "Grant, my boy. Have a seat." He waved the glass toward the chair next to him in front of the hearth.

Accepting the invitation with gratitude that he wouldn't have to face the bedroom and Katie for a while, Grant sat.

"Join me?" Alfred held the bottle of brandy aloft.

At first, Grant considered Alfred's offer. Maybe a wild-eyed, mind-numbing drink would help his nerves. On second thought, facing Katie in the morning presented its own difficulties. He didn't need a hangover to contend with, too.

"No, thanks."

"Suit yourself." Replacing the bottle on the end table at his elbow, Alfred took a long sip of the amber liquid. "You get thrown out of your bedroom, too?"

The question took Grant by surprise. "Too?"

A chuckle, imbued with alcohol drifted to him from Alfred. "Yup. Harriet's ticked at me. Told me she doesn't want to share her room—*her* room, mind you—with a welcher."

"Welcher?"

"Yup. Says I welched on my duties as a husband and a host." He punctuated each word with his glass. The liquid sloshed perilously close to the rim.

Alfred was smashed, and if not smashed, well on his way.

"She thinks I'm a juggler." He nodded vigorously, agreeing with his own statement.

"Juggler?" Grant was having more than a bit of difficulty keeping up with Alfred's erratic train of thought.

"Yup. She thinks I should be able to balance my private life with my social life with my romantic life." He turned to stare at Grant, blinking several times, presumably trying to bring Grant into focus. His inebriated boss waved the glass again and this time, brandy sloshed over the edge onto the carpet. "Oops. Best clean that up or she'll have something else to nag me about."

When Alfred appeared not to be able to rise from his chair, Grant laid a hand on his arm. "I'll get it." He bent and swabbed at the damp spot with a cocktail napkin, while wondering how his boss had gotten into such a state.

"I'm telling you, my boy, that woman does nag with all the precis...presh...with all the—"

"Precision?"

"Right. What you said. She does it with all the preshishon of a drill sergeant." He swung toward Grant, nearly losing his drink.

Grant eased it from his hand and placed it on the table out of Alfred's reach. Alfred slumped back in the chair and ran his hand wearily over his eyes.

"Sometimes, I wish I'd become a carpenter. The money's not bad and I'd have had a life, and then Harriet wouldn't have had anything to bitch about."

"Harriet doesn't want you to be a lawyer?" Grant couldn't recall noticing any strong objections from Harriet about what Alfred did for a living. But then, he didn't live with them, either.

Alfred erased the words with an unsteady wave of his hand. "It's not the legal profession she objects to, just the time I have to spend at it." He glanced around him at the room filled with antiques, some first editions, genuine leather furniture and polished wood. "How does she think we got all this? The good fairy?" He giggled at his analogy.

Grant blinked. Had that giggle come from his boss? He couldn't believe it, but then, that seemed to be par for the course for the past few days. Little had happened that made much sense.

"I'll tell you where it came from," Alfred continued, his words slurring even more than before, his voice rising in volume.

"Sir, the ladies are sleeping." The last thing either of them needed right now was contending with two irate females.

"I'll tell you," Alfred began again, his voice a hoarse whisper. "It came from hours of work. Hours, my boy. It came from sacrificing myself for my family, for Harriet, to give them the best of everything." He sat back in his chair, his face nearly disappearing behind the brown leather wing. "I gave it all to them. Everything I could—cars, homes, clothes, vacations to Europe, educations." He swung toward Grant unsteadily. "I'd say I was a darn good husband and father." He threw up his hands. "What more does that woman want from me?" Alfred peeked expectantly around the chair's wing. "Well?"

Grant grabbed the first answer that came to mind. "Well, sir, maybe you should make the effort to spend more time with her. That might solve everything. She does love you and no doubt wants to have you around more, do things with you, even if it's just sitting at home in front of a fire—" Grant's words came to a sudden end.

Was that what Katie was trying to tell him? No. Harriet and Katie couldn't be compared. Apples and oranges. Harriet didn't resent Alfred's work, just the time it took from her.

Katie, on the other hand, hated anything to do with the law and his career. She'd made that abundantly clear from the time they'd first talked about his aspirations for his future in law. In fact, it was the night before she'd walked away from him at college that she'd made her hatred of his chosen profession known. The night he'd lost Katie.

Besides, his and Alfred's circumstances couldn't be compared, either. Alfred never knew what it was like to do without. Grant did, and he wasn't about to do it again as long as he could help it.

A loud snore came from the chair beside Grant. Alfred had fallen asleep. Quietly, Grant rose, turned off the lamp, placed the fire screen in front of the hearth, then slipped from the room.

Back upstairs, he stood at the foot of the bed and gazed at Katie. The moonlight played over her face, turning her flaming hair to dark silver. Her hand laid curled next to her cheek, giving her the innocent air of a child at rest. But Grant knew that beneath those covers lay a real, warm, flesh-and-blood woman. A woman who could raise his blood to the boiling point, both in anger and in passion. And right now, looking down at her and fighting every physical urge in his body to slip into the bed beside her, anger was the last thing on his mind.

Shaking his head to rouse himself from his sensual stupor, he moved to his makeshift bed on the couch. Glancing back at Katie, he knew sleep would be elusive at best. Gathering up the pillows and the blankets, he headed for the stairs that led upward through the turret to the widow's walk atop the house.

The night had remained warm. It would be like camping under the stars. Grant stepped onto the square, platformlike porch atop the roof. Looking around him, he understood why, in days of the three-masted ships, women watched from places like this for the return of their men from the sea. From here he could see miles across the dark water, all the way to where a row of dark clouds lay across the horizon.

He moved close to the hip-high railing surrounding the walk and watched the movement of the clouds to see what direction they were going. Heading south. He wouldn't have to worry about them spoiling his impromptu camp-out.

He spread the blanket so he could look out over the Atlantic and then lay down, prepared to spend a night in wakeful wondering about the woman downstairs. As he gazed heavenward at a sky scattered intermittently with clouds and stars, a strengthening, westerly breeze ruffled his hair.

DISTANT POUNDING awoke Katie. She sat up and listened. The noise came from the top of the stairs leading to the widow's walk. The wind had probably blown the door open. She'd closed it once already tonight.

Climbing from bed, she shuffled up the stairs and pulled the door closed. About to turn away, she decided she'd better make sure she didn't have to make another return trip. Deftly, she slid the bolt in place, then plodded back down the stairs to her lonely bed.

Casting a glance at the sofa, she frowned. Where was Grant? The bedside clock read 2:20. Oh, well, he was a big boy and she'd lost enough sleep over him.

She flopped into bed, pulled up the sheet and closed her eyes.

GRANT FELT something wet on his face. One drop. Then another. He bolted to a sitting position. Seconds later, he was drenched by the storm that had blown in from the sea. Clutching his blanket around him and grabbing his pillow, he headed for the door. He turned the knob and pulled. The door wouldn't budge.

He tried again and again with the same results. The damned door must be stuck. Fisting his hand, he began pounding on the wood.

"Katie! Katie, let me in. Katie!"

Nothing.

He began banging anew. "Katie! Dammit, woman, wake up. I'm getting soaked. Open the damned door."

Still nothing.

"Katie! Open this door!"

Thunder rolled overhead. Out to sea, streaks of white fire slashed through the boiling sky. The wind whistled around the housetop, pummeling him with water. Rain poured over his head and down his back in cold sheets of never-ending torture. He shivered. Clutching the soaked blanket closer, he pounded on the door.

"Dammit, Katie. Please, open the door."

Nothing.

"Katie!"

Still nothing.

Dragging in a deep breath, he screamed her name again. "Kaaatttiiieee!"

Suddenly, the door burst open, nearly knocking him over. He stood face-to-face with not only Katie, but also Alfred and Harriet. All three people gaped at him, obviously expecting an explanation for why he was on the top of the house in a howling storm.

While Alfred and Katie stood transfixed, Harriet grabbed his arm and tugged him inside to the cramped landing. "What on earth were you doing out there in the rain?"

Grant threw Katie a glare. "I couldn't get the door open." He swiped angrily at the water dripping off his nose and ears.

"Odd. We've never had trouble with that door before." Alfred checked the knob. Turning it, he swung the door open with ease. "Seems to be working okay now. Maybe the rain swelled the wood."

"Alfred, it was locked. Now, let's get Grant downstairs and into some dry clothes, before he catches his death." Harriet took his arm and steered him toward the top stair.

Grant didn't believe the swollen wood theory for a moment. He glanced at Katie. She had her hand over her mouth and the glimmer of glee in her eyes told him she was putting up a valiant fight to keep from laughing out loud. His blood boiled.

In the bedroom, Harriet hurried off to get Grant a towel. Katie flopped on the end of the bed and stared at him, her hand still hiding her amusement at his predicament.

"You locked the door," he accused. "You locked me out there."

She nodded, not trusting herself to remove her hand. Grant had spent more time in water in the past few days than a fish. This time, though it had been totally unintentional on her part, she couldn't help but be pleased that in some strange way, she'd gotten back at him for acting like an ass about his job. Too bad some of his white-collar clients couldn't see their ace legal counsel now.

"Admit it. You locked that door on purpose."

"How was I to know you were playing Boy Scout?" she finally managed to say, but nearly lost it again when a large drop of water ran down his nose and just hung there before dropping to the carpet.

"Right. Like I'm going to believe that. You knew it was going to storm and you saw me go up there, so you locked me out to get back at me for—" He stopped and looked at Alfred and Harriet who stood near the door, as if ready to make a quick escape.

"Well, Harriet dear, perhaps we'd better go back to our room so Grant can change." Alfred took the towels from his wife, then handed them to Grant. "You'll find dry bedding in the top of the dressing room closet." Taking her elbow, he steered Harriet from the room. The door closed softly behind them.

"You can admit it now"

"Admit what?"

"That you locked—" He paused in his tirade to eye her lace teddy appreciatively.

Damn! Her robe was gaping open.

With as much dignity as she could muster, she stood and walked to the side of the bed. She'd ignore him. She slipped the robe off and whipped back the bedcovers, slid into bed, then flopped back and jerked the sheet to her chin. "The truth is I had no idea you were up there. The wind kept blowing the door open. I locked it to make it stay closed. Now, if you don't mind, I think I'll go back to sleep. That is, if you're finished playing Aquaman." She paused and stared at him. "Why were you up there?"

"Never mind." Wrapping the blanket around him, he tossed the soggy pillow on the floor, then headed toward the bathroom, nearly falling on his face when his feet got tangled in the folds of clinging, wet material. He looked like a Roman senator who had taken a bath with his toga on.

Katie held back the laughter threatening to burst forth again. A small squeak escaped her pursed lips.

"Not funny, Donovan."

"Waverly," she corrected, before she could stop the words from spilling from her mouth. Why in hell had she said that?

For a long time, Grant stood in the doorway looking at her, then he smiled and stepped inside.

Exactly what did that lecherous smile mean?

Great.

Just what she needed. Not only would she lose sleep trying to vanish visions of him the last time he'd been soaked to the skin and what had happened as a result, but now she'd have to figure out exactly why he felt it was so funny that she'd put her mouth in gear before she'd engaged her brain.

The bathroom door swung open. "For the record, I don't believe a word of that explanation." He started to close the door, then stuck his head around it. "By the way, Mrs. Waverly, that little yellow scrap of lace…very sexy." He winked, then closed the door.

HARRIET EASED their bedroom door shut behind her and her husband. "See? I told you these children need Katie's mother here." She peeled off her wet robe and laid it carefully over her dressing table chair to dry. "Locking the poor boy out in a storm." She clucked her tongue and shook her head.

"They probably had a spat again, and she was trying to teach him a lesson. I don't see that that means we need to call in the National Guard." Alfred held his head and spoke just above a whisper.

Since she'd gone looking for him hours ago and found him and his bottle of brandy in the library, Harriet knew her husband had gotten a bit tipsy. Time enough in the morning to nurse the fool through his hangover. Right now, she had things to do, and the only way she could get them done without interference was with Alfred safely asleep.

"My poor Alfred, why don't you just lie down, dear, and we'll talk about this in the morning." Carefully, she eased him back onto the pillows, then pulled the sheet up to his chin. Before she'd made it across the room, snores emanated from the sleeping man. She saluted her reflection in the dressing table mirror. "Way to go, Harriet."

Getting a dry robe from the closet, she donned it and then slipped out of the bedroom.

Downstairs, she turned on the kitchen light and picked the receiver off the wall phone. Punching in a series of numbers, she waited.

"Hello. Information? Please give me the number of Elizabeth Donovan in St. Augustine, Florida."

During the photo session in the garden, Grant and Alfred had come out to sit on the patio to watch. Harriet had noticed how Katie's spirits had sunk even lower at the sight of her husband. And now this latest development had made Harriet certain of her decision. Despite what Alfred thought, this girl needed her mother.

First thing in the morning, she'd call Katie's mother. Elizabeth could arrive by tomorrow afternoon—and perhaps, as an extra treat, she could convince Katie's brother to join them, too. What was his name? Charles. She would insist Elizabeth bring Charles. Maybe they could do something about saving Katie and Grant's marriage.

As a taped voice recited a series of numbers to her, she jotted them on a pad. Pleased, she hung up the phone, tucked the piece of paper in her pocket, then flipped off the light switch.

BREAKFAST THE NEXT DAY held all the gaiety of a funeral procession. Katie stared out the window at something only she seemed able to see. Harriet took her residual anger at Alfred out on a bowl of batter containing, to Grant's way of thinking, some very suspicious lumps. Grant wished he were anywhere but on an island in Maine with a woman who wouldn't give him the time of day and another who was bent on giving him acute indigestion.

"Good morning." Alfred's voice rang out in the quiet breakfast nook like the bells in Saint Patrick's Cathedral on Easter morning. How, after the night he'd put in, could the man be so disgustingly cheerful?

"Morning." Katie's and Grant's voices blended into one. Harriet's remained conspicuously absent.

Glancing at his boss's wife, Grant noted a slight smile playing at her lips. A bad feeling, having nothing to do with the three lumpy pancakes Harriet placed in front of him, invaded the pit of his stomach. Picking at a lump with his fork tine and finding a plump blueberry buried beneath the dough, Grant sighed in relief and reached for the butter at the same moment Katie did.

"Excuse me. You first," she said pulling her hand away as if scalded by boiling water.

"No. Go ahead." He waited while she spread the butter over her pancake, then replaced the dish in front of him. He hated this silence that hung between them, but he had no idea what to do about it.

"Alfred and I will be going to the mainland for supplies this morning." Harriet took a seat across from her husband and smiled at him.

"We are?" Alfred's dark, thick eyebrows elevated

a few inches into what would have been his hairline, if he had hair. "This is the first I've—" He stopped dead when Harriet threw him a look. "To the mainland. Of course. Now I recall." He dove into the pile of pancakes.

"Do you want us to go with you?" Was that hope Grant detected in Katie's question? Hope that she wouldn't be trapped here alone with him all day?

"No, dear. You and Grant busy yourselves here. Alfred and I are bringing back a surprise for you and, if you see it, well…it won't be a surprise, now will it?" Harriet smiled at Katie and patted her hand.

"A surprise?" He and Katie exchanged wary glances.

Grant didn't need any more surprises. He'd had quite enough of them ever since he'd found out he was married to Katie. One more unexpected occurrence might be his undoing.

"Yes, dear. Now, do eat your breakfast. I have to get these dishes done before we can leave. Elmer will be most put out if he has to wait."

"I'll take care of the dishes, Harriet. You and Alfred just run along with Elmer." Katie dropped her gaze to her plate.

"Why, thank you, Katie. That would be very helpful."

"Speaking of thank you, I have one I'd like to add to that." Alfred wiped his mouth on his napkin and leaned back. "You did me a great service last night, Grant, with that little chat we had. I do believe your advice was right on the money."

"Advice?" Katie asked, her fork halfway to her mouth.

"Grant caught me in a…shall we say, morose state of mind—"

"—more like inebriated," Harriet interjected, frowning at her husband.

Alfred frowned back. "—*morose* state of mind last night in the library and we had a wonderful talk." He turned directly to Harriet. "You'll be interested in this, Harriet. What Grant advised me on will have a direct bearing on our lives."

"Oh?" Harriet laid down her fork and gave her husband her full attention.

"He told me that I should spend more time with you and less in the office. I think he's absolutely right." He patted her hand. "I've not paid nearly enough attention to you, my dear."

Harriet glowed. "Oh, Alfred, how sweet."

Katie frowned, then glared at Grant. Grant avoided direct eye contact with her. How in hell would he explain this? After the argument they'd had yesterday about the importance of a job versus family and the stand he'd taken, this would have to be handled delicately.

Not long after breakfast was finished, Grant found himself alone with a very upset Katie.

"What was that all about?"

"What?" His innocent act gave him a grand total of about three seconds to find an answer to her question.

"The advice you gave Alfred. Why is that good for him and Harriet and not for us?"

He looked at her imploringly. "Katie, think about it. Alfred has made his career. I'm still climbing the ladder. He's got all the things I want for us."

"No, Grant, all the things you want for *you*. I never asked for anything beyond your love and time." Katie poured dish soap in the sink.

"Why don't you use the dishwasher?"

She turned a look on him that could have melted steel.

"In the sink is good. Just making a suggestion."

"When I want your suggestions, Grant Waverly, I'll ask for them."

He held up his hand and grabbed a dish towel from the rack beside the sink. "Fine."

"Fine."

As he took a plate she'd rinsed from the rack, he glanced at her face. Moisture streaked her cheek. "Katie, are you crying?"

She shook her head. She'd be damned before she let him know that the advice he'd given Alfred had injured her more than anything he could have done. How could he so easily see the very thing she'd been trying to drum into his thick head with someone else's relationship, but not with theirs? Why was she wasting her time on the damned man? Why couldn't she just let go and walk away?

Suddenly everything that had happened over the past few days got to her. She bent forward, resting her head on her soapy forearms. Sobs rose from deep within her, sobs that had spent seven years gaining in volume and strength.

"Oh, my Katie."

She felt Grant's arms slide around her. Guided by his hand, her head came to rest in the crook of his neck. He held her close and murmured soft assurances in her ear.

"Don't be nice to me," she whispered between sobs. "Please don't be nice."

Gently, Grant swiveled her chin around, until their lips were a mere breath apart. "I have to," he whispered. "I can stand anything but watching you cry, seeing you hurt. I never wanted to hurt you."

She stared into his dark eyes. She could see her reflection in their depths. For once, she believed him. He hadn't set out to hurt her. He had his idea of what life should be like, and she had hers. Unfortunately, neither of them could see beyond that.

"There's no hope for us, is there?" he asked, his voice thick with emotion.

She wanted to say yes, but she couldn't. She knew it, and so did he. "No. I don't see that we can ever get past our differences."

"Then give me something to keep after you walk away this time." He looked down at her.

With just a slight nod, she brought her lips to his. What started out as a quick kiss soon grew. Before she knew it, Katie was clinging to Grant, desperately trying to hold on to him in some way.

Together, they moved toward the stairs.

THE SOUND OF the boat's motor roused Katie from sleep. She moved, only to find herself trapped beneath Grant's leg. He hadn't heard the boat, nor felt her move.

"Grant, wake up." She shook his bare shoulder. "The Biddles are back."

Grant opened one eye and smiled at her. "Hi."

"We don't have time for cordial greetings. We have to get dressed."

"Why? The Biddles will understand." He gave her a rakish grin.

Katie climbed out of bed, dragging the sheet with her to cover her nudity. "Maybe they will, but I won't."

She didn't want to explain to him that having the Biddles see them looking as if they'd just gotten out of bed, which they had, would serve only to remind her of things she didn't want to think about right now. Like how their afternoon in bed had only made things harder for her. Or that she had to tell both them and Grant that she'd be leaving the island as soon as possible. Or that she'd been wrong. That walking away this time would be the hardest thing she'd ever done in her life.

Hurrying into the bathroom, she got dressed. When she came out, Grant was dressed and looking out the window. "They have someone with them. Wonder who it could be."

"Maybe they decided to bring another one of the junior partner candidates and his wife here," she offered. Katie didn't care. All she wanted was to get out of this room with the rumpled sheets and scattered clothes. She wanted to forget the past few hours and how her heart had betrayed her brain again. Maybe that way she could make her break clean and painless.

"Let's go downstairs." She strode toward the door. Behind her, she could hear Grant's low words.

"Running away again, Katie?"

Ignoring him, she headed for the top of the stairs. When the front door swung open, she had one foot on the top stair. Glancing down into the lower hall, she gasped, clutched the mahogany railing in a white-knuckled grip, and stopped so fast that Grant bumped into her back.

Standing inside the hall, smiling up at her, was Harriet's promised surprise.

Chapter Ten

"What in hell are Charles and your mother doing here?"

Grant's hoarse whisper came from above Katie on the staircase. She couldn't answer. Though she tried to move and speak, her feet remained frozen to the top step, while her brain worked to assimilate what her eyes were seeing in the hallway below.

He nudged her side. "Katie?"

Shaking away the stupor, she tilted her face away from her mother, the Biddles and her ex-fiancé, Charles. "How should I know?" she murmured, then turned back to the group below and smiled sweetly.

"Sweetheart." Lizzie held her arms out to her daughter, as if she hadn't seen her in years, much less the three days since they'd left Florida. "Give me a hug."

Katie hadn't heard her mother use that tone since her only child skinned her knee roller-skating. Then there was that protective look in her mother's eyes....

With another nudge from Grant, Katie mobilized her body and slowly descended the stairs.

Lizzie hurried forward to meet her daughter, arms outstretched. Her gaze fastened on Katie, then shifted to Grant. She engulfed her only child in her embrace. "My poor, sweet baby." Then in a low whisper, she added, "What's going on?"

Smiling at Charles and taking in Alfred's discomfort and Harriet's pleased-as-punch expression, Katie hugged her mother back. "Mother, what a surprise." Then she answered Lizzie's whispered question. "How in blazes do I know? Just play along for now."

"Harriet said you needed me," her mother said for all to hear, then under her breath she added, "I didn't have the heart to tell the woman that you'd been doing quite well on your own ever since you crawled out of your crib at eighteen months."

"Katie?" Harriet stepped forward. "Hadn't you better save some of those hugs for your brother, Charles?"

Katie swallowed hard. It looked as if the proverbial cow dung had hit the fan.

Lizzie whirled in a circle looking for, Katie surmised, the child she didn't know she had.

Charles stared at Harriet like a deer caught in oncoming headlights.

From the staircase, she heard Grant's gasp of surprise. She threw him a we'll-discuss-this-later glance.

Harriet and Alfred seemed the only ones who took the announcement without the danger of coronary arrest. Harriet must have shared with Alfred the conversation she'd had with Katie in the rose garden. However, Katie hadn't remembered to tell Grant about the little white lie concerning Charles's being her brother.

Could things possibly get worse? Of course they could. Whatever made her think this madness would ever end?

Lizzie positioned herself between the Biddles and Katie and whispered, "We need to talk, my girl."

"We will," Katie whispered back impatiently. Plastering a smile on her lips, she sidestepped Lizzie, walked to Charles and dutifully placed a chaste kiss on his cheek. "Charles, how nice you could come with Mother."

"Yes. Nice," he mouthed, his eyes still glazed over with shock.

She had to get her mother and Charles alone before any more was said. "Harriet, would you make us some coffee, while Grant and Alfred take the bags upstairs? I'm dying to show Mother and Charles the view from the front porch."

"Certainly, dear. Alfred, put Lizzie's things in my room...you and Charles can share our grandchildren's...I've already moved your things in there... well, we can't very well ask the young marrieds to give up their bed, now, can we?" she said, when Alfred raised a questioning eyebrow. "Katie, you take our guests out to the front porch...I'll bring the coffee directly...Alfred, do be careful not to scratch the luggage on the hall table...there's a dear." Harriet disappeared into the dining room.

Not waiting for a second invitation, Katie linked

her arms in her mother's and Charles's and steered them out to the porch.

"KATHLEEN, I hardly think lying about who I am is going to get Grant his job. That *was* the reason for this entire exercise, wasn't it?" Charles had recovered nicely from his recent shock, but not his indignation. "You could have at least warned me about my new status as your brother."

Glaring at him, Katie smiled sweetly. "I would have, Charles, if I'd known Harriet planned on dragging you out here."

Katie hadn't expected Charles to take the news of his sudden blood relationship to her easily, but neither had she expected him to be totally unreasonable. She'd already explained to him how this mess had come about and she wasn't about to do it again. But he couldn't seem to see past his upset to the core of the problem—Grant's job.

"Cool it, Chuck," Lizzie interjected. "You aren't making things any easier. Having gained you as a son isn't my idea of the perfect family, either, but you don't see me complaining."

Charles huffed. Katie wasn't sure what contributed more to his attitude, Lizzie's statement, the predicament he found himself in, or her mother's use of his hated nickname. And she didn't have time to either shush her mother or placate Charles. "Charles, will it hurt you just to play along for a while?"

"Personally, I think it's all quite amusing." Lizzie giggled.

"Mother, puleeze!" Katie glared at her, cutting her mirth short.

Charles folded his arms across his white golf shirt. "I can tell you, I'm not happy being part of this fabrication, Kathleen."

Like she hadn't figured that one out on her own already. "And I suppose you think I've been having a party since I got here." The Irish temper Katie tried to keep in check began raising its volatile head. "Good grief, I've been running in circles since my feet hit that dock three days ago."

Charles leaned forward, then arched a reproachful eyebrow at Katie. "Then why not just tell everyone the truth of the matter and save us all a lot of nerve-racking tension?"

What was the truth? She'd lost sight of it long ago.

Even though she'd just made the same suggestion to Grant, Katie couldn't bring herself to reduce Grant's dream to ashes. And even though she'd never share that dream with him, she had to make Charles see that he couldn't blow the whistle on them.

The idea that she cared if Grant got his promotion stunned her momentarily.

"Here we are." Harriet came through the door, followed by Grant and Alfred. "I thought this called for a bit of celebration, so I brought us a special treat."

She set the tray on the table. Katie looked down at a large plate of fresh fruit and a bowl of rich, dark chocolate dip. Red, ripe, domestic strawberries bordered the centerpiece of the fruit tray. Katie stared at them in numbed silence, recalling things she wanted desperately to forget.

"Well, doesn't this look scrumptious," Charles announced, taking a strawberry and slowly dragging it through the chocolate dip. He bit the berry in half and discarded the remainder to the small plate Harriet had provided for the green stems.

Grant stepped forward. "You're wasting most of the berry, Charles." Laying his hand on Katie's shoulder, he selected a berry and coated it with the melted chocolate. "There's an art to eating strawberries. I'm surprised you didn't know it. Your *sister* recently taught it to me. Let me demonstrate. Katie, you'd better watch me to make sure I have it right. If you recall, I'm rather new at this."

She recalled all right and she didn't want any part in this demonstration with its sexual overtones. But, Grant stepped into her line of vision. Holding Katie's gaze, Grant bit the berry the way she'd taught him on the island.

Katie sucked in her breath. Hot and cold flashes careened over her. Her heart stopped, then began again, its beat strong enough to echo in her ears. She glanced around, certain it could also be heard by everyone present, but they were all intent on Grant. All his attention centered on her, silently asking for things she couldn't give, demanding answers she didn't have and staking a claim to which he had no right.

Quickly looking away, her gaze collided with Charles's. He studied her with marked interest. Several times, he looked from her to Grant. Charles's features suddenly softened, startling her. She'd never seen that expression on him before. He nodded briefly, then smiled.

"I think I understand, now," he said.

Everyone assumed he meant the strawberry-eating technique, but Katie felt his statement had nothing to do with the fruit and everything to do with her. This whole damned mess was becoming too much for her. Suddenly, she yearned for her life the way it had been before Grant had charged into it again—simple, uncomplicated, predictable, secure—all the things she never had with Grant.

"Excuse me." She stood. "I need my shoes." Barefoot, she padded across the porch toward the French doors.

Getting her shoes meant one thing to Grant. Katie was about to crawl back into her safe cocoon. His Katie was about to disappear and a gut fear told him, if he didn't stop her, this time he'd lose her for good.

"I'll help her find them," he announced, then hurried after her.

"KATIE," Grant said, catching up with her in their room. "What's going on? "

Flopping on the edge of the bed, Katie stared beyond the turret windows. "Harriet thought I needed my mother here because she found me crying in the rose garden the day we came back from the island. She called my mother and then Charles. Until they walked through the front door, Harriet and Alfred were the only ones who thought he was my brother. It came as as much of a shock to them as it did to us.''

''I don't mean that and you know it.''

She glanced at him, then quickly turned away.

''Now that Charles is here, what will happen to us?''

''Nothing *can* happen.'' Presumably to avoid looking at him, she picked at a small loop of thread in the seam of the bedspread. ''I want my old life back, and I want you gone.'' Her voice cracked.

Grant couldn't just let go. He had too much at stake. ''Gone?'' He walked closer, but he stopped when she flinched away. His heart twisted painfully in his chest. He was losing her. He could feel it. ''You want me gone after what happened yesterday and today?'' he asked, trying to keep the desperation from his voice.

She turned to stare hard at him. ''No. I want you gone *because* of what happened.'' Standing, she moved away to the windowsill and sat. Centering her gaze on the expanse of blue ocean beyond the window, she sighed. ''Before you came back into my life, I had everything I wanted.''

''Everything?'' He hoped she wasn't going to try to convince him that she'd loved Charles. He knew Katie too well. When she gave love, it was with every fiber of her being. The woman who had made love with him yesterday and again today could not have loved someone else. Had that been true, she would never have consented to share a bed with him.

"Everything that would make me happy." She looked up at the white clouds floating in the bowl of blue sky. "I suppose I have no one to blame but myself. In three short days, you turned my whole world topsy-turvy. I let you do that. I could have fought you and refused to try to help you get your job, but I didn't. Maybe I didn't because deep inside, I thought that there might be a way…" Her voice faded into silence. She shook her head as if to clear away the thought.

She didn't have to finish what she'd started to say. Grant knew in his heart the rest of the sentence.

"I've come to a decision. If Charles will forgive me and forget this entire week, I'm going to marry him."

For a long moment, Grant stared at her, unable to allow her words to penetrate his brain. She couldn't possibly mean this, not after yesterday, not after today, not after…

The sunlight framed her head in a halo, making her red hair glow with a light of its own. Her green eyes glistened with unshed tears. Her bottom lip trembled. But her face never lost its look of determination.

With all the cataclysmic strength of an earthquake, her words slammed into Grant's heart. He'd lost her again—and for the same reason he'd lost her the first time.

She glanced at him. He searched her face for some small sign that she'd relent if he just said the right words. Her expression was blank, emotionless. Ironically, the lack of emotion tore his heart open and made him face the seriousness of her words. "I'm sorry, Katie. I had no right asking you to pretend, to come up here and lie to these people. It's time they knew the truth."

Katie's gaze snapped to his. "You're going to tell them about us?"

He nodded, not trusting his voice to speak.

"When?"

"Tonight. After everyone has gone to bed, I'll talk to Alfred."

"But what about your job?"

A sarcastic laugh broke from him. His job. Funny, but it didn't seem to matter anymore. Nothing mattered anymore in the face of losing Katie. In the short span of a few days, he'd managed to screw up his own life and hers. But he didn't matter anymore. Out of all of it, the one thing that did matter was that Katie would be walking away again—this time for good.

"I guess I'll just have to take my chances."

"It won't change my mind," she warned.

That hadn't occurred to him, but had it, he would have disregarded it. He nodded. "I know. This is just something I have to do. Maybe then I'll be able to live with myself again." He laughed. "Who knows, maybe Alfred won't care. Maybe all this has been for nothing. Maybe he'll keep me on in the firm."

And maybe hell will freeze over, too.

GRANT HAD BEEN GONE from the bedroom for a long time before Katie allowed herself to think about what she'd done.

What *had* she done?

She'd taken a bath in reality. Grant would never change and she'd been fooling herself by believing he would. That little demonstration on the porch had been like a blinking neon sign. Charles was content with half the strawberry, while Grant had to have it all. Nothing could have brought it home to her with more clarity. She'd been an idiot to think otherwise. Charles embodied everything she desired in a man.

Then why did it hurt so much? This *was* what she wanted, after all. A settled, stable life with a man who loved her and would work at making their marriage a happy, shared union.

Still the pain continued to slice deep into her heart. She felt as if she'd severed a limb. Clutching at her middle, she staggered to the couch and bent double with tears. She let the pain pour from her, hoping, when it was all over, she'd be cleansed, free, at peace.

"Are you okay, Katie?"

Katie barely heard the door close behind her mother. She couldn't push an answer past the tears filling her throat.

"Grant just came downstairs and walked off toward the other end of the island. Poor man looked like a criminal who'd just been given the—" She placed a hand on Katie's shoulder. "Sweetheart?"

Seconds later, Katie was engulfed in her mother's loving embrace. "What is it? What's been going on here?"

"Mama," Katie sobbed. Pulling away from her

mother's shoulder, Katie looked at her mother through a blur of tears. "It's all such a mess."

Pulling a handkerchief from her pocket, Lizzie dried Katie's tears. "Now, tell me about it."

Taking the handkerchief, she blew her nose. "I was so stupid. When Grant showed up, I started feeling all those things I'd felt in college. I thought—" she hiccuped softly "—I thought that this time..." Sighing heavily, she leaned back against the couch, resting her head on it and staring at the ceiling. "It doesn't really matter what I thought. I was wrong."

"You thought you could change him?" Lizzie brushed a wet strand of hair off her daughter's forehead.

Katie nodded, then smiled at her mother. "You know, when Harriet said she brought you here because she thought I needed you to talk to, I laughed." She kissed her mother's cheek. "I was wrong. I do need you."

A smile lit Lizzie's face. "That's the first time in ages that I've heard you say that. I'm glad. I like you needing me."

Grabbing her mother's hand, Katie squeezed it. "What do I do?"

"Follow your heart."

Katie stood and walked back to the window. She sat on the wide sill and looked beyond the ocean vista to a future without Grant. "I tried that and look where it got me." She turned to her mother. "I want to have the man I love around. I want him to put his family first and his career second. I want a happy marriage. Not like you and daddy had. Is that so bad?''

''Unhappy? Your father and me?'' Lizzie raised her eyebrow, then left the couch to sit on the side of the bed, facing Katie, who was still slouched on the windowsill. She took her daughter's hand in hers. ''Where ever did you get such an idea? Your father and I had a wonderful marriage. In the beginning, we traveled some very rough ground, but most newlyweds do.'' She smiled. ''And, as some newlyweds do, we almost didn't make it.''

''You and Daddy?'' Katie was stunned. To her surprise, she'd never thought of her parents' marriage as shaky, despite her father's long absences and her mother's loneliness. ''When he was home, you always seemed blissfully happy. It was only when he was away…''

''Your father was a salesman, Katie. There is no job in the world that takes a man away from his family more than that.'' Lizzie frowned at her. ''Don't you remember, when he missed his train home, the nights we waited supper for him and the times, when you had something at school, that he didn't show up?''

Katie recalled those times vividly. It was precisely because of those memories that she wouldn't settle for being married to a man who put his job first. She remembered her mother's tears, and her own, the lonely nights when it seemed like her father had forgotten them. They'd watched the clock, finally giving up, and she'd gone to bed to lie awake and hate herself for caring. Then, he'd come home the next day and she'd forgive him. But as the years passed and his pattern of absences continued, Katie found it more and more difficult to forgive.

"They were lonely times for all of us." Lizzie smiled wanly. "You have no idea how he hated being away. But he had to earn a living, and what better way than by doing what he loved? Oh, I could have tried to change him, but if I had, he wouldn't have been the man I fell in love with. So I learned to live around the absences. We made the times together so special that pretty soon the times when he wasn't there didn't matter quite so much, because I knew, when he did come home, it would be wonderful." She brushed a speck of lint from her navy slacks. "I don't think you've ever reconciled yourself to that aspect of our lives."

Katie turned to stare down at her mother. "I remember how much I hated him being away and how lonely you were. But I knew Daddy loved us. I never doubted that."

"Didn't you? If that's true, then you'd have no trouble understanding that a man can love his family and his career equally. That one doesn't forego the other."

"Mom, love is not the problem, don't you see? I don't want to spend my life waiting and lonely, like you did. Or even worse, ending up in a divorce court because I've found that living without him is no lonelier than living with him." She paused. "You know how I feel about divorce."

Lizzie stared past Katie's shoulder. "I know you've never approved of my three recent marriages. I often wondered why. I won't pretend to have that one figured out." Lizzie held up her hand to stop Katie's words, then pushed herself up to pace near the window. "But it doesn't matter, because, in the past few months, I've figured out why I married those men. I had been so very happy with Colin Donovan that I thought it was a simple matter of finding that happiness again with another man. But I was wrong. I can never replace your father. And after watching you, I realized that *caring* is no substitute for real love."

Lizzie made her way toward the door. "I'll see you downstairs at dinner."

Katie reached out a hand to her mother. "Mama, what do I do?"

"That, my dear girl—" Lizzie touched the center of her chest "—is between you and what's in here."

GRANT GAZED OUT out the living room window onto the front lawn of The Homeplace, thinking how the activity taking place outside resembled a summit conference. In the corner of the yard closest to the pool, Katie and Lizzie sat on a bench in deep conversation. On the opposite side, in Harriet's treasured rose garden, she and Charles walked. But from the serious expression on both their faces, they were not discussing roses.

"Why aren't you out there with the rest of them?" Alfred came and stood beside Grant.

"I needed some time to myself." He wasn't about to tell Alfred that he'd spent the past half hour trying to form the words to explain the lie Katie and he— no, not Katie. She was an unwilling participant in this charade he'd perpetuated, the lie he had devised to secure his job with the firm. However, the right words had remained just beyond his grasp.

"Well, I'm glad you didn't go out there. I want to talk to you." Alfred moved away and sat in one of the leather winged chairs. "Join me." He gestured to the other chair.

Grant did as Alfred suggested, but not without butterflies of apprehension taking flight in his stomach. "Sir?"

"Alfred, my boy. I asked you to call me Alfred."

Grant smiled. "Alfred." His boss's name felt strange on his tongue.

"I just got a call from Daniel Hoffman."

Wondering what Biddle's second in command could want, Grant waited.

"He told me the board took a vote on the junior partnership, and you were named." Alfred reached to shake his hand. "Congratulations, my boy."

Forcing a smile to his lips he didn't feel, Grant shook Alfred's outstretched hand. Odd. He waited so long to hear those words and had expected it would be the greatest day in his life. He should be elated, jumping for joy, shouting at the heavens. Instead, he felt as if he'd just been given a death sentence. "Thank you, sir...Alfred."

Great! After years of work and planning, after demolishing his personal happiness, he'd achieved his goal. But without Katie to share it, the goal had become hollow and meaningless.

Alfred's bushy brows drew together into a deep frown. "You don't seem pleased."

Grant forced a smile to his lips. "Oh, but I am. Very pleased," he lied. "This is something I've waited a long time for." The right words poured from Grant's lips, but only pain poured from his heart. He'd lost Katie. Nothing mattered anymore. Least of all this job.

"I have to tell you that my vote, while being *aye*, was tentative."

"Oh? Why is that?" Grant couldn't care less, but he knew Alfred expected the inquiry, so he voiced it.

"I want to make certain everything between you and Katie is settled, before I make it a positive endorsement for your taking the job." He leaned forward. "Of course, I didn't tell Daniel that." He grinned. "Just between you and me, Daniel can be worse than a gossipy old woman when told a secret. We on the board make certain that he's the last to know anything."

Grant opened his mouth to tell him that things would never be better between him and Katie, because there was no him and Katie. But he snapped it closed. Later, after dinner, he'd tell Alfred the truth, then let the chips fall where they may. After dinner, when the pain had lost its razor edge.

FROM ACROSS the dining room table, Katie studied Grant. Something was bothering him. He'd barely said two words since they all sat down to eat. Could he be feeling the pain of their separation, too? Fool! More than likely, this preoccupation stemmed from his having to face Alfred later with the truth. However, the way he kept looking at her made her wonder if perhaps her first conclusion hadn't been right. Could he be regretting…

She quickly dismissed any concern for him on that score. If he was upset, it wouldn't last long. Grant had a capacity for putting anything that bothered him far from his mind so he could concentrate on his career. He'd done it seven years ago, when he'd allowed her to walk away, and he could do it again. In a few days, he'd be back in Miami, knee-deep in court cases. Katie Donovan would be the last thing on his mind.

That satisfied her. She'd do the same. As soon as she'd had a chance to talk to Charles alone, they'd again start planning their wedding—that is, if he still wanted her.

While she was sure Lizzie's words of wisdom had been intended to make Katie see that she shouldn't try to change Grant and that she should pursue a relationship with him, they had worked exactly the opposite. She was more sure than ever that Charles was the right man for her. She would *not* live as her mother had, no matter how happy she'd professed to be. Katie had seen the tears and disappointment.

Katie's only need was happiness—the kind that comes from a mate who's there for you—always. Not

the storybook kind she'd had in college and for the
past few days with Grant. Storybook romances had
no substance, no basis in reality, and the end result
was an empty bed and an aching heart. What she felt
for Grant was nothing more than some fantasy her
subconscious had been clinging to for seven years.
Actually, she should thank Grant for these three days.
They'd really opened her eyes and made it possible
for her to move on with her life. Now, all she had to
do was convince her heart.

The tinkling of silverware against glass roused her
from her thoughts. Alfred had called for everyone's
attention.

"I have an announcement to make."

"Sir, could we wait on this?" Grant looked worried. He threw an apprehensive glance at Katie.

"No, my boy. My motto is when you have good
news, share it with those around you."

Grant sat back in his chair and lowered his gaze to
his lap.

"I had a phone call this afternoon from my law
partners and they have unanimously voted to give
Grant his junior partnership in the firm." Alfred
raised his wineglass. "To Grant, the newest junior
partner at Biddle, Hoffman and Henderson."

Harriet rushed over to embrace and kiss Grant.
Lizzie smiled and patted his shoulder. Charles voiced
his congratulations, then looked at Katie.

Katie managed to avoid looking at Charles, but
Grant's drawn face captured her attention. Why
wasn't he jumping up and down? He'd waited a life-

time for this day. Slowly, she stood and rounded the table to his side.

"Go ahead, my dear girl," Alfred coached, "give your husband a kiss. He's earned it. It's not every day a man gets all he's ever dreamed of."

Grant stood and rested his hands on her hips. "Congratulations, Grant. I know how badly you've wanted this."

Leaning forward, she brushed his lips with hers. A jolt of raw pain arrowed through her. "I mean that," she added, looking deep into his dark eyes.

"I know you do. Thanks." His voice lacked the enthusiasm it should have had. Reluctantly, Grant released her, but his gaze followed her as she moved back to her seat on the opposite side of the table. Not until Katie had settled in her chair did he allow his legs to fold under him. Thank goodness the chair was still there to cushion his collapse.

In the library, the telephone rang.

"I'll get it," Alfred said, then left the room.

"Grant, you don't seem terribly pleased with your promotion," Harriet pointed out. She and Charles exchanged knowing glances.

Forcing a brightness to his face, Grant smiled broadly. "On the contrary, Harriet. Why wouldn't I be pleased? I've always wanted this. It's the fulfillment of a lifelong dream. What more could I want?" His gaze drifted to Katie. "I'm very grateful to everyone who made this possible." A smile curved her full lips, but pain reflected in her eyes. Blinking, he turned away quickly.

"Indeed, what more could you want?" Charles said. "A lovely wife, a successful career...life can be very good to us sometimes."

"Yes, sometimes," Grant mouthed, his gaze fastening once more on the woman across the table from him, who looked as if she'd just been dealt a lethal blow.

Alfred reentered the dining room. His eyes smoldered. His gaze burned into first Katie, then Grant. His cheeks glowed with rage. His mouth cut a tight, straight line across the lower half of his face.

"Alfred, dear, what is it? Bad news?" Harriet rose and rounded the table to stand beside her husband. She took his arm, but he shook it away.

"Harriet, please resume your seat."

Obviously stunned by her husband's tone, Harriet did as he'd ordered.

"This seems the evening for surprises," Alfred announced. He stared from Grant to Katie, his brows forming a deep V. "I just had a very interesting conversation with a Mr. James from the FBI. It seems the security check wasn't quite finished when they sent us their report. There were still a few threads they had to go over." He paused as if waiting for someone to reply.

"Threads?" Harriet said.

"Yes, my dear, threads. It seems that because the marriage license bureau in Las Vegas had recently received calls from Grant Waverly and Kathleen Donovan Waverly to verify their marriage, they did some further investigation." Alfred's gaze burned into Grant's. "Some new information has come to light."

Grant glanced at Katie. She blinked and paled slightly. He began to squirm in his seat. Had Alfred somehow found out about their lie? The bottom fell out of Grant's churning stomach. He would do anything to spare her this humiliation.

"Alfred, can we speak about this in private?"

His boss glared at him, the rage becoming more and more evident in his face. "We will speak about it now! You had no problem living this lie. You should have no problem facing the consequences of your actions."

Alfred's words effectively silenced any further protest from Grant. He sent a speaking glance at Katie, hoping this wouldn't be too bad. She smiled wanly. They both looked at Alfred.

"I've been asked to convey to you that Mr. Donaldson of Las Vegas, Nevada, had neglected to maintain his ministerial license. The marriage between one Grant Allis Waverly and one Kathleen Maureen Donovan is a shameful fraud!"

Chapter Eleven

After Alfred's announcement about Grant and Katie's marriage being a fraud, the shocked silence in the dining room deafened Grant. Everyone found their voices at once, then all hell broke loose.

"Alfred, this is not funny!" Harriet glowered at her husband.

"Hell's bells," Lizzie crowed.

"That's impossible!" Katie's and Grant's voices rang out in unison.

"I spoke to the man in the license bureau myself." She looked around the table from one face to another, as if searching for confirmation that her entire life had not been disrupted for nothing.

Charles alone remained silent, seemingly in deep thought.

"Alfred, how could you say such a thing?" Harriet surged to her feet. Her outrage transformed her quiet beauty.

He glared at his wife. "Because it's true. My staff double-checked before they called me. Do you think

I'd make something like this up for our amusement, Harriet?''

Grant searched for the words to argue Alfred's announcement. ''I don't understand,'' he finally managed to say.

''It's all very simple. The man, who performed the ceremony, never renewed his licence. He was not legally qualified to marry you. Ergo, your marriage wasn't legal.'' Alfred's face and neck turned bright crimson. His features remained set and immovable.

Grant looked at Katie. His mouth quirked in a half grin. ''Irony?'' Katie's expression told him she did not find this amusing, but if he didn't laugh at this bizarre situation, he'd go insane sometime in the next few minutes.

Katie stood and placed her hands on her hips. ''Grant, do something.''

''What would you have me do?'' Hadn't he done enough already?

''I want an explanation,'' Alfred demanded.

Briefly, Grant related the background on their staged Las Vegas wedding. ''It was never supposed to be real to begin with, then you told me that the security check had found I *was* married.'' He cast a look at Katie. She'd directed her gaze at Alfred. ''I wanted that job, so I talked Katie into pretending we had been happily married for seven years.''

Lizzie's laughter sounded stringent to his ears.

''Mother!''

''Oh, Katie, where's your sense of humor? This sounds like something from a B-rated sitcom. You couldn't have pulled this off better if you'd planned it.''

Chastising her mother's outburst with a quelling glance, Katie looked back at Alfred.

Alfred continued to glare first at Grant, then Katie. Obviously, he didn't see the amusement in this that Katie's mother did. Grant didn't, either, but he was really beginning to like Lizzie. When she got to be that age, the old Katie would have been just like her. Somewhere along the line, Katie had forgotten how to laugh at life—not that either of their lives were particularly humorous right at the moment.

"All this, then, was to no avail," Charles finally stated flatly, a sadness filling his expression. Then he looked at Katie, whose gaze rested intently on Grant. "Then again…"

Grant ignored them all and apologized to Katie with his eyes. He would have given a lifetime of successful court cases to have prevented her going through this embarrassment.

"Alfred, could there have been a mistake?" Harriet sounded on the verge of tears.

Grant smiled inwardly. Harriet, always trying to smooth the waters, ever the arbitrator. Well, this time Harriet couldn't smooth the waters, and as far as arranging peace between Grant and his boss, one look at Alfred's furrowed brows and burning gaze told Grant that was far beyond even Harriet's talents. Not that it mattered. What mattered was to clear Katie's name of any part in this sham he'd gotten her involved in.

"Katie had nothing to do with any of this. It was my idea entirely."

"That's not totally true, sir." Katie's gaze locked with that of a glowering Alfred Biddle. "I could have stopped it, but I didn't. I went along willingly."

Grant, stepped in before she could say more. "That's not so. I blackmailed her into going along with me. She refused, but I told her if she wanted a divorce, she'd have to pretend to be my wife until I got the promotion."

"Blackmail." Alfred's frown deepened, if that was possible.

Slamming her hand on the table, Harriet raised her voice above the rest. "Will someone explain to me what's going on here?"

"Harriet, kindly stay out of this." Alfred glared at his wife until she sank submissively into her chair, her mouth drawn in a tight line of rebellion. He turned back to Grant. "You do realize what this means?"

Slowly, Grant nodded. "Yes, sir, I do."

"We cannot have a man holding a position of importance in the firm if he cannot be trusted to be totally honest with us. Nor can we condone such unethical practices as blackmail by one of our employees."

Swallowing hard, Grant nodded again. In the space of a few seconds, he'd gone from junior partner to employee to unemployed and oddly enough, he didn't care. "Do what you want to me, but please don't hold Katie accountable for any of this."

Eyes wide, Katie shook her head. "Grant, I—"

"No, Katie. It was my idea. I'm not going to allow you to shoulder any of the blame for this."

"But your job—"

"—I'm afraid there are no jobs for Grant at our firm," Alfred stated.

"Alfred!" Harriet's eyes had taken on the size of small moons.

"Stay out of this, Harriet." Alfred leveled a glare at his wife that would have cooked rocks.

"There are other jobs." Grant eyed his ex-boss, daring him to challenge his words.

Alfred cleared his throat, then raised his chin a notch higher. "Not without a recommendation from Hoffman, Biddle and Henderson."

Another gasp of outrage came from Harriet's end of the table.

"Then I can start my own practice. I'm a good lawyer, Alfred, and I don't have to depend on you and your uptight firm to get clients. My track record, as you once said, speaks for itself." Grant turned to Charles and extended his hand. "Charles, my sincerest apologies for anything that's happened in the past few weeks. I have a feeling, if you talk to a certain Katie Donovan, she may have changed her mind about your marriage."

"Marriage?" Harriet was on her feet again before Charles could say a word. "Katie can't marry her brother."

Lizzie hid a new gale of laughter behind a snowy linen napkin.

Throwing her mother a speaking glance, Katie tried

to explain. "Charles is *not* my brother, Harriet. I'm afraid this part of the misconception *is* my fault. I had to explain to you the identity of that man I kissed at the country club and saying that he was my brother seemed the easiest. Charles and I were engaged to be married when Grant came to me with news that I was his wife. Well, he *thought* I was his wife."

"But…you…he…the island…" Collapsing into her chair, Harriet gave up the attempt to form a coherent sentence and just stared openmouthed at Katie.

"I broke the engagement the night before Grant and I were marooned on the island."

A sigh issued from Harriet. "I'm confused." Her gaze darted around the table. "They're married, but they're not married…ministers without licenses performing weddings that aren't really weddings… relatives who aren't really relatives…brothers engaged to sisters." She stood, her hand pressed to her forehead. "I think I'll go lie down for a while."

Watching Harriet's retreating form until she disappeared up the stairs, Grant turned back to Katie and Charles. "I'm sure you have a lot to discuss."

Charles nodded, then took Katie's arm, steered her into family room, then through the French doors. Katie glanced back at Grant one time. Grant's heart broke in two. Through his own stupidity and selfishness, he'd lost the only thing in the world that mattered to him. He slumped back in his chair.

But it wasn't entirely over until Alfred delivered the final blow. "I'll expect your resignation on my desk as soon as you get back to Miami."

He nodded and stared absently after Alfred as he strode toward the library. Grant didn't even want to think about the law firm. He was too busy trying to imagine life without Katie beside him. He'd gotten exactly what he deserved, but even that didn't make the prospects of a future alone any easier to bear.

He glanced out the window at Charles and Katie embracing at the edge of the rose garden. Tears blurred the vision.

KATIE PLACED the smallest piece of her luggage next to the pile Elmer was to take to the boat. The residue of the evening before still clung to her mind. Poor Grant, he'd ended up with nothing. Her heart twisted at the thought. He could be an insensitive jerk, but surely he didn't deserve this.

She shook her mind loose of such thoughts. Thanks to Charles being so understanding, she was once more an engaged woman, and as such, she should be thinking about her fiancé and her wedding.

The wedding changes Charles had insisted on still raised some questions in her mind. Why had he insisted on moving the wedding date forward to this month? Maybe he didn't want her to go roaming off again before they were husband and wife. After all, he'd said he wanted her with him as soon as possible. His demand chased some of the chill from Katie's bones. That's what she wanted—a man who viewed his marriage and family as top priority. Why, then, did her heart feel as if it had shattered into a thousand pieces?

Even the fact that Grant didn't seem to mind that Alfred had fired him didn't bring her any sense of relief. Knowing Grant, he'd simply move on to the next law office and start his ascent up the success ladder again. One word Grant didn't have in his vocabulary was *quitter*. Even when faced with possible defeat, when he finally set his mind on something, he rarely turned away from his goal. It was one of the traits that made him so good at his profession.

"Katie?"

She spun around at the sound of Grant's voice. His appearance pained her. He wore a suit and tie again— the lawyer.

"I'll be leaving from the boat dock in Rockland to fly to Boston," he said in answer to her unspoken question. "There's an old friend of mine there who's been after me to join his firm. I may take him up on it." Grant half smiled. "Good chance of advancement. There're only three guys in the firm."

The confidence Katie had always heard in Grant's voice had returned. He was ready to scale the next mountain on his way to success. Her heart shattered just a little more.

"Good luck." She extended her hand. When his palm engulfed her fingers, she had to consciously keep from pulling back from the heat that zipped up her arm and straight to her heart. Would she ever get over this silly college crush?

"Thanks. You, too. Charles seems like a really nice fella, once he lets down that stiff veneer of his."

"Yes. He is a good man. I'm sure we'll do well

together.'' Before her gaze veered off to study the Chippendale desk in the corner of the hall, it met his briefly.

Do well? Grant thought. Not ecstatically happy? Just *do well?*

For a split second, he considered dragging her into his arms and reminding her of the passion they'd shared, showing her what she should expect and deserved from marriage, but he mentally stepped away from such thoughts. He'd blown his chance with her. He might as well get used to the idea of Katie in another man's arms, Katie sharing kisses with another man, Katie sleeping in another man's bed.

Deep inside him an arrow of acute pain veered through his gut.

"You folks ready?" Elmer stood in the doorway, his knee-high boots dripping water on the porch floor.

"Is my mother at the dock?"

"Ayuh." Elmer reached for the largest suitcase.

"Then I'm ready." Katie looked at Grant. "How about you?"

"I'll be going on the second trip with Harriet and Alfred. There's no room for me this time." Or ever, he amended silently.

Katie stared at him for a long moment, then seemingly on impulse, leaned forward and kissed his cheek. "Goodbye, Grant," she whispered, then slipped out the door behind Elmer.

"Goodbye, my Katie," he whispered to the empty doorway, his fingers going to caress the spot where her lips had lingered so briefly.

WHEN KATIE REACHED the dock, Charles was already there talking to Harriet. As she strode toward them, they ceased their conversation and smiled at her. Had she been a suspicious person, she'd have guessed they were up to something. However, at the moment, rational, logical thought was far beyond her capabilities. She couldn't erase the vision of Grant from her mind.

"Ready, darling?" Charles took her arm and guided her down the ramp to the float. Harriet followed close behind.

"I'm so very sorry things didn't turn out differently," Harriet cooed.

"They turned out for the best," Katie soothed her troubled hostess. Discussing the past few days simply depressed Katie, so she tried to steer Harriet away from it. "Will you and Alfred be leaving, too?"

"Yes, dear. We'll be on the next boatload with—" Harriet stopped, throwing an apologetic look at Katie.

Katie patted her hand. "You can say his name. Grant already told me he'd be going to the mainland with you and Alfred."

"I'm just so peeved at Alfred. He should have been here to say goodbye to you." She clucked her tongue disapprovingly. "After all, he is the host and hosts have duties no matter what else has happened...isn't that right, dear...of course it is...if I were his mother, I'd ground him...that's what I'd do...ground him."

"Harriet. Please. I fully understand why Alfred isn't here. He has every right to be angry."

"Goose feathers. The man has to learn to unbend, roll with the flow."

"I think that's roll with the punches or go with the flow." Charles smiled at his frustrated hostess. His cheeks glistened with the fine salt mist that clung to his skin.

"Whatever. The man has been like this as long as I've known him. Black is black and white is white and there are no shades of gray. Well, it's about time someone gave him a lesson in the color wheel." She patted Katie's hand and grinned. "And I'm just the one to do it." She glanced at Charles and flashed him a smile. "Don't you worry, dear. I'll fix everything."

Katie shook her head. "There's nothing to fix."

"Boat's leavin'," Elmer called from the end of the float where he'd begun untying the lines.

"Goodbye, my dear. Please don't forget to stay in touch." Harriet hugged Katie close.

"I will. Goodbye." Katie stepped onto the boat with Charles's help. He followed, then waved to Harriet.

Elmer slipped the remainder of the ropes from the cleats, threw them aboard, then climbed back on the boat. He pulled himself up the ladder to the flybridge and a few moments later, the boat slipped away from the dock. Katie stayed on the stern and waved at Harriet until the boat started to make the turn toward the mouth of the cove.

Just as she turned to go inside the cabin where Lizzie waited, Katie caught sight of a lone figure standing on the porch of The Homeplace. *Grant.* He raised his hand and waved. Katie waved back. Then the boat rounded the point and he was lost to her view.

Stepping inside the cabin, Katie looked at Charles. She had made the right decision, hadn't she? She cast a glance over her shoulder, but it was too late. Grant was gone. This time for good.

"Trust me, Katie. It'll all turn out for the best." As always, Charles held her hand. Ever protective, ever attentive, ever present Charles. Charles, who instinctively knew how to make her happy.

AFTER CHARLES LEFT the cabin and climbed the ladder to sit on the bridge with Elmer, Katie settled beside her mother on the settee in the main salon.

"So, Charles was your choice?" Lizzie asked.

Dragging her attention to her mother, Katie stared in awe. "I didn't know you had taken up crocheting," she said, fingering the bright-yellow yarn her mother had taken from a canvas tote bag at her feet.

"Keeps my mind off the rocking of the boat." Lizzie deftly worked the crochet hook in and out of the stitches, amazing Katie with her dexterity.

This definitely was not a recently acquired talent. She ran a palm over the strip of rainbow colors intricately worked into a complicated pattern of leaves and flowers. When had her mother started crocheting? Had she paid so little attention to Lizzie that she'd missed this?

"Well?"

"Well, what?"

"Is Charles your choice?" Lizzie stopped working long enough to throw Katie a quizzical look.

"Yes, Mother. Charles is my choice."

"So, we're back to Mother again, are we? That explains a lot."

"Meaning?"

"Meaning, you're thinking with your blasted brain again, Katie Maureen." Lizzie laid her yarn in her lap and frowned heavily at her only child. "What happened to making your decision based on what you feel is right?"

"Marrying Charles *is* what I feel is right." Katie reached for the ball of yarn that had dropped from Lizzie's lap and started to unwind across the cabin floor.

"Poppycock!"

She paused in replacing the yarn. "What's that suppose to mean?"

Lizzie took the yarn from her daughter and tucked it back in her tote bag. Weaving a strand of yarn around her finger, she resumed work on the half-finished motif taking the form of a carnation. "I don't believe for a minute that this comes from your heart. Are you selling yourself a bill of goods again?"

"Of course, it comes from my heart." Katie sighed. This conversation was going down the same old road. "Could we change the subject?"

"Very well. Let's talk about your father and me."

"What about you and Daddy?"

"I think I may have given you the wrong impression the other day. Our lives were not all roses. There were times when I hated our situation so much, I thought I'd go crazy. I even left him once to save my sanity. Or so I thought." Lizzie snickered.

Katie stared at her mother openmouthed. "You left Daddy?"

Her mother nodded, keeping her eyes on her crocheting. "When you were about three. I was headed straight for a divorce court. I couldn't stand the lonely nights anymore." Lizzie paused. When Katie opened her mouth in shock, Lizzie went on. "We were separated for almost three months. You were too small to remember, but I never cried so much in my life as I did during those three months."

She dropped her crocheting to her lap and stared out the back of the boat into the past. "I hated being away from the man I loved and who loved me. By punishing him, I punished myself, and you even more." She shook her head, as if to dispel the memories of that unhappy time. "Finally, I went back to him. I realized that being totally without him was infinitely worse than being without him between his selling trips."

Just then, the boat hit a deep swell, causing it to dip and then rise on its watery bed. The dishes in the small galley rattled behind their secured doors. The curtains at the windows swayed and danced. Lizzie groaned. Just as the boat gained a level attitude, it hit the next swell. Lizzie groaned again. She placed her crocheting back in her tote bag.

Katie was stunned. Her mother and father separated? "Daddy loved you," was all she could say.

Pressing her hand to her stomach, Lizzie nodded, then shook out a musk-scented handkerchief to dab at the sheen of moisture collecting on her forehead. "If you'd stop kidding yourself—" she swallowed hard "—you'd see that Grant loves you, too."

Katie watched the receding image of the island. "Grant loves his work more than he'll ever love any woman." When no reply came from her mother, Katie turned to look at her. Lizzie's skin had paled considerably and had a decidedly green cast to it. "Are you all right?"

"I'm going to live, if this blasted boat ever stops rocking. And you're changing...the subject—" She covered her mouth with her hand, then slowly eased it away. "I still think, for a woman who hates the idea of divorce, if you marry Charles, you're flirting with a decree and—" Lizzie's eyes grew very large. She pushed past Katie, then lunged for the back deck.

Katie followed quickly. She found her mother leaning over the rail. Holding Lizzie's hand, Katie wished she could rid herself of the hopeless, empty feeling in the pit of her stomach as easily as her mother was ridding herself of her seasickness.

She glanced up, across the wide expanse of desolate ocean. When Charles had asked her to marry him again in the rose garden, she'd been so sure, so very sure that she had made the right decision. Now, thanks to her mother, doubts buffeted her mind again. Doubts about herself and Charles and Grant.

Shaking them away, she forced her mind to concentrate on the beautiful antique wedding gown hanging in her closet at home and how good Charles was to her and how much he cared for her. And how they'd have a good life together. And...how Grant had already started planning a life without her.

Chapter Twelve

"Boss? You wanted to see me?"

Grant stood before his office's large picture window overlooking downtown Miami. Hypnotized by the waves rolling into the shore in the distance, he'd been remembering another shoreline and other waves and—

Abruptly, he swung away from the window and the memories. Ray stood just inside the door in his usual disarray, munching on an Oreo. "Yes. I wanted to say goodbye."

His paralegal looked around at he packed boxes sitting on Grant's desk, chair and sofa. "So the rumor's true, huh? You got canned." He shook his head. "Ain't gonna be the same around here without you."

Grant shoved one hand deep into his jeans pocket, then pointed at the remainder of the cookie Ray munched on. "Got another one of those?"

Shock registered on Ray's features. He blinked. "Ah...sure." Pulling a second cookie from his pocket, he dusted off the lint, then handed it to Grant.

Raising the cookie in a toast, Grant grinned. "Here's to my new firm."

Ray's forehead creased, pulling his eyebrows into a deep V shape. "Your new firm?"

Taking a bite, Grant chewed for a while, then swallowed. "I've decided it's time I went out on my own." He sat on the windowsill. The cold marble had warmed slightly in the afternoon sun. He pushed open the casement window and breathed deeply the salt-scented air. Memories threatened to bombard him of another time when he'd breathed the scent of the ocean. He shook them away.

"You hiring yet?"

Grant gazed at Ray. He was serious. "You looking for a job?"

"You offering me one?"

"Sure, but it's not gonna be easy. Long hours. Not much pay to start with."

Ray laughed. "Like I'm becoming independently wealthy working here. Besides, money isn't everything."

For a long moment, neither of the men spoke. Grant thought about what Ray had just said. "No, it isn't." Some things were much more important than how much a person can buy. Unfortunately, he hadn't learned that in time. He blinked away the phantoms and concentrated on Ray. "If you leave here and work for me, this paycheck may seem like a fortune."

"Like I said, money's not everything." He sauntered to Grant's desk and flopped into the swivel desk chair. "Hell, the only reason I put up with this bunch of old fuddy-duddies was because of you. Once you're gone, so am I. I might as well go with you, if I can.''

Smiling, Grant rose and extended his hand. ''Thanks, Ray. The job's yours, if you're sure you want it.''

Ray pumped his hand with enthusiasm. ''I'm sure.''

''Mr. Waverly?'' Grant's dark-haired secretary—former secretary—called from the office doorway.

''Yes, Mandy?''

''Mr. Biddle would like to see you in his office, right away.''

Ray raised an eyebrow. Grant shrugged. ''Thanks. I'll be right there.''

''Whadda you suppose he wants? One last shot at you?''

Popping the remainder of the cookie in his mouth, Grant picked up his jacket, started to put it on, then stopped. ''I guess my mode of dress won't matter anymore.'' He shoved the tails of his shirt into his jeans.

''That's something we need to discuss about this new job. The dress code stuff. Am I gonna have to wear a suit coat and be careful of my cookie crumbs?''

The first note of real humor Grant had felt in days slipped past his lips. ''Ray, you're the only job applicant I know who considers Oreos a job perk. Tell you what, I'll personally see that your supply of cookies never runs out.''

Ray's face blossomed into an ear-to-ear grin.

Grant grew serious. "Thanks for sticking with me. I appreciate it." Too many people had left him lately and it gave his battered ego a real boost to know that someone still believed in him—even if Katie didn't.

Don't go there, Grant told himself sternly.

"No problem." Ray drew another cookie from his pocket. An impish grin spread over Ray's face. "Here. Show the old man your stuff."

Grant took the cookie, twisted the top off, licked the white filling, then sauntered out of the office.

"NOW, WHEN GRANT comes in here, Alfred, you let me do the talking."

Alfred arched an eyebrow at Harriet. "As if you'd allow otherwise."

"Shush, I hear him coming." She fluttered about the plush office, too nervous to stand still straightening chairs and fluffing plant leaves. "Oh, this is so exciting."

"I have no idea how I allowed you to talk me into this. It's crazy. What makes you think Grant will go along with it?" Alfred shuffled a stack of papers and glared at his wife over his reading glasses.

"Because he's a very levelheaded, sensible young man. That's why." She threw him a look that dared him to argue with her conclusion. She hadn't gone to all this trouble to let Alfred throw a monkey wrench into the works now. People were depending on her.

"Alfred, never in our married life have I ever resorted to holding sex over your head to get my way.

However, I'd strongly advise you to keep your word on this issue or your bed is going to take a decidedly Arctic plunge in temperature. Do I make myself clear? Mess this up and you, my good man, will be sexually grounded."

Alfred opened his mouth to answer, but the door opened.

They both turned toward it. "Grant, dear. How nice to see you."

Grant stood just inside the door and smiled as Harriet placed a light kiss on his cheek. The soft scent of her perfume lingered in a cloud around him. "Hello, Harriet." He glanced at his former boss, who began shuffling papers. A diversion Alfred often used to keep from confronting an uncomfortable situation. "Alfred."

Alfred nodded curtly. "Grant."

"You wanted to see me?"

"I'm afraid I'm to blame for giving that impression. I wanted to see you," Harriet said. She moved about, seemingly more nervous than normal. "It's about Katie."

Grant's nervous system went into alert. "Katie? Is there something wrong? Is she hurt?" His gaze darted from Harriet to Alfred.

Harriet rushed to his side and patted his arm. "No, dear, nothing like that."

Heaving a sigh of relief, Grant collapsed in the large leather chair opposite Alfred's desk.

"Before I have my say, Alfred has something he'd

like to ask you.'' She cast a commanding glance at her husband. ''Go ahead, Alfred.''

Alfred glared at Harriet, then turned to Grant. ''You have no idea how lucky you are that the marriage was a sham,'' he said in a hushed tone. He threw his wife a speaking glance. ''Once they marry you, they think they can dictate your life, personal and professional.''

Grant couldn't argue with that. He'd have given his life for that marriage to have been real. And he'd give anything to have Katie running his life for him, just as long as she was in it.

''After speaking with my wife—'' Alfred squirmed for a moment ''—I have reconsidered your employment at the firm. If you want it, your job is still here with us.'' He cleared his throat uncomfortably. ''That's not to say I'm not still disappointed with your behavior.''

''Can it, Alfred...dear.'' The look Harriet leveled on her husband oozed saccharine sweetness.

Looking from Alfred to Harriet, Grant wondered just how much this wonderful lady had to say in this offer Alfred was making. ''I appreciate the offer, sir, but I've already made other plans.''

''Oh, dear!'' Harriet fanned herself with her handkerchief and collapsed into the chair next to Grant's.

''Well, if you've already—'' Alfred began.

''Alfred!'' Recovering quickly, Harriet shot to her feet and glared at her husband.

Throwing his wife a sideways look, Alfred sighed.

"Grant, this woman is not going to give me one moment's peace unless you come back to work here."

The prospect of Alfred spending the remainder of his days with Harriet gnawing at his psyche appealed to Grant. He smiled. "I'm sorry, sir. My mind is made up. I spent a good deal of time in Boston thinking about this. I want to work for myself, build my own firm."

He turned to Harriet. "Now, what was it you wanted to talk to me about?"

GRANT STIRRED the cream into his coffee. He waited for Harriet to return from the powder room of the small restaurant to which she'd steered him after they'd left Alfred's office. When she'd insisted on having their "chat" somewhere away from the hustle and bustle of the firm, he'd almost said no, but she'd smiled so pathetically, he hadn't had the heart.

She reminded him of the sad-faced doll he'd seen in the window of a toy store he'd wandered by while in Boston. He'd stopped and stared at all the toys for a long time. He still couldn't figure out what he'd seen in that window that had changed his mind about joining Jim's firm. Whatever it had been, his decision to go it on his own had flashed through his mind and he'd felt, gut deep, that it was right.

Now that he'd made the decision, he felt really good about it. Like he'd done something in his life for once that didn't have a dollar sign attached to it. Oh, he knew the going would be rough, but he suddenly relished the idea of struggling, of making something for himself. Something with his stamp on it, something that he'd built from the ground up.

It came to him then what had made him change his mind. A small red wagon in the corner of the toy store window. The same kind of wagon he'd wanted for Christmas the year he'd turned six. Of course, he'd never gotten it. They hadn't had enough money that year for frivolous toys.

But he'd gotten something better, something that, now that he was grown up, he could look back on, something that shined brighter than any red wagon ever made.

His grandfather had come from the West Coast to spend the holidays with them. He'd lavished his small grandson with presents. Everything from airplanes, to toy soldiers, but no wagon. But beyond the presents, his grandfather and his parents had lavished him with love. More love than he'd ever be able to hold. It had turned out to be one of the happiest Christmases of his childhood.

When his grandfather flew home, he remembered crying at the airport and begging him not to go, but he did, amid promises to return the next year. Grant had gotten angry and refused to kiss his grandfather goodbye or to tell him he loved him. Several days later, his grandfather had passed away quietly in his sleep.

Until that day in front of the toy store, Grant had forgotten that Christmas, and the love. He'd forgotten that nothing's absolute. Sometimes you lose people, and sometimes they leave and never come back. He'd forgotten the guilt caused by his rash behavior at the airport. He'd forgotten how much he wished he'd said the words and given his grandfather that hug.

More important, he'd forgotten that happiness doesn't come with a price tag, that it's measured in smiles and not in dollar signs.

Then he started thinking about his life and how he'd spent so many hours trying to get to the top of the heap. What really stunned him was when he started wondering why.

He had wonderful memories of his childhood, but somehow, he'd forgotten the good ones and only remembered the disappointments, the things he had to do without. He'd pushed the Christmas memories to the back of his mind and to the bottom of his agenda chart, right above starting a life with Katie.

Success would never have given him back the love he'd had that Christmas long ago, nor would it have guaranteed his and Katie's happiness.

Katie understood that. She'd asked him why he thought his parents were poor when they were rich in love. Why hadn't he seen that before it was too late? Before he'd lost Katie. If he could only undo those few days with her, go back and live it over, he'd tell her that nothing mattered but them. He'd dig ditches, if she asked. He'd—

"I'm sorry I was so long, dear. There was a line halfway around the building." Harriet slid into the chair next to Grant. "Did you order?"

"Just coffee." He slid her cup closer to her, then handed her the cream and sugar.

She added both liberally to her cup, then gave it a quick stir. The dark brown liquid transformed to beige. "I do so enjoy coffee in the afternoon...can't have too much in the evening...it keeps me awake, then Alfred complains that my tossing and turning keeps *him* awake." She glanced at Grant.

He grinned, finding he liked listening to Harriet chatter on. Her endless talking gave him a sense of permanency and oddly, of continuity. As if, as long as Harriet chattered, the world would keep turning.

Fluttering nervously, Harriet patted the ruffle of her pink blouse, then smoothed the sleeves of her navy jacket. Her movements disturbed the cloud of perfume surrounding her, wafting it to Grant as well as the people at nearby tables. The essence of Harriet touched everyone in one way or another.

"I'm sorry to go on so. I do wish they hadn't left this part to me. I always talk too much when I'm nervous. But not to worry. I'll be fine." She moved the salt and pepper shakers, positioning them precisely in the middle of one of the larger squares in the check tablecloth.

What could Harriet possibly have to be so nervous about?

"DID YOU PICK UP your dress from the dressmakers?" Katie asked.

Lizzie glanced at her daughter, then back at the porcelain figure cradled in the palm of her hand. She smoothed her thumb across the face of the woman.

Behind the counter of her antique shop, Katie bent

to fuss with some boxes that had slid off the shelf beneath the cash register. Once sure they wouldn't slip to the floor again, she straightened to find her mother still staring fixedly at the Victorian knick-knack. "Lovely isn't it? We just got that in yesterday. It came from an estate auction up the river."

Lizzie jumped at the sound of her daughter's voice, as if she'd just woken from a dream. "What?"

"I said, we just got the figurine—"

"No, not that. You asked something about my dress."

"Did you remember to pick it up from the dress-makers?"

"Yes, last night. I stopped on my way home." Lizzie's reply was somewhat vaporish, as though she had no idea what she was talking about and the objects of her thoughts lay miles from the antique shop.

"Mother?"

"What?"

"Are you all right? You aren't going to get ill again, are you?"

Frowning at her daughter, Lizzie set the figurine on the counter. "Good grief, Katie. That was because I was on that blasted boat. I don't usually get seasick on dry land." She huffed a gust of air that moved a wave of hair lying on her forehead. She sniffed. "Smells musty in here. You should leave the door open and let in some fresh air."

"Mother, even you know that the damp sea air isn't good for antiques. The room is full of old things. Besides, the air-conditioning is on." Wise to her mother, Katie knew Lizzie's evasion tactics very well. "What is wrong with you today?"

Snapping her gaze to Katie, Lizzie studied her for a moment. "Nothing's wrong. Why do you ask?"

"You've done nothing but fidget since you came in the shop. You seem preoccupied, in another world."

Standing, Lizzie walked to a small candle table and ran her fingers over the wood. "I'm fine. Just deep in thought."

"Oh?"

She turned to Katie and made an impatient face. "I can think without you giving me a hard time, can't I?"

Touchy, touchy. Maybe the rushed plans for the wedding had finally gotten to her, too. It wouldn't surprise Katie in the least. She'd been strung out all week, snapping at Charles, impatient with everyone around her.

Between trying to get the wedding together, the store inventoried, her assistant briefed for the time when she and Charles would be on their honeymoon, and pushing the constant intrusions of Grant Waverly from her thoughts, this hadn't been a week she'd want to repeat right away. Never would be soon enough.

Before Grant could take a foothold in her thoughts, Katie directed her attention back to Lizzie.

"Is it the wedding?" she asked her mother's back, dreading the result of her question and the argument that would inevitably follow. However, anything was better than fighting off the memory of the night on the island with Grant.

"As a matter of fact..." Lizzie faced Katie. "It is the wedding." She walked back to the counter and took Katie's hand in hers. Katie could feel the softness of her mother's palm against her skin. A comforting feeling. "I want to apologize for being such a harridan about your marriage to Charles. I had no right to try to force my opinions on you. You're a big girl and deserve the right to make your own choices."

Katie felt her mouth drop open. "You mean you're finally giving us your blessing?"

"I'm giving your wedding and the man you'll spend your life with my love and my good wishes. If that's my blessing, then yes, I'm giving you my blessing." She leaned forward and kissed Katie's cheek. "I'm certain you'll be happy."

Skepticism filled Katie's mind. Lizzie didn't do a turnaround out of the clear blue sky. Once her mind was made up, little besides an act of God could change it. She stared at her mother's sincere expression, looking for the flaw, the one tiny thing that would tell her Lizzie had either gone stark raving mad or she was up to something.

"Why the change of heart?" Katie watched her closely.

Glancing at Katie, Lizzie busied herself with the figurine she'd set down moments earlier. "Why not? You tried to make it with another man, and it seemingly didn't work." Lizzie replaced the figurine. "Charles and I had a lovely chat over coffee after you came back to the shop. I have to admit, I underestimated him. He's got a good head on his shoulders. I can see now that he's a very bright man. Very observant." She leaned forward and kissed Katie's cheek. "I have to run."

Stunned by her mother's change of heart, Katie could only stare after her retreating figure.

"See you tonight." Lizzie swung open the door. The bell over her head tinkled softly.

"Tonight?"

"You haven't forgotten the rehearsal dinner is at seven?"

Katie shook her thoughts loose. "No. Of course I haven't forgotten."

"Well, don't dawdle here too late. You know how Charles likes to be on time." Lizzie slipped out the door.

Katie watched her mother climb into her car, then drive away. Although Katie felt relieved that her mother had changed her mind about Charles, unease clung to her mind. It simply wasn't like Lizzie to trade horses midrace. If Katie knew her mother, Lizzie was up to something, and it probably didn't bode well for anyone—especially Katie.

THE ORGAN MUSIC SWELLED. The pounding in Kate's temples increased. Sunlight streamed in a dizzying rainbow through the stained-glass windows. The fragrance of the gardenias in her cascading bouquet permeated the air, the heavy perfume upsetting her already queasy stomach even more. Her hair, piled in a Victorian coiffeur atop her head, felt like a lead helmet. Her veil trapped her in a pocket of oppressive heat. Absently, she wondered if all brides felt this bad on their wedding day, or if she'd set a new precedent.

She glanced at her mother. Lizzie, inordinately happy, looked lovely. Her pale blue dress mirrored her lively eyes, and her snowy hair had been arranged in a crown of curls. On her shoulder a white orchid stuck its purple tongue out at Katie, as if mocking her. Despite her quavering emotions, or because of them, Katie smiled, glad that she'd asked her mother to escort her up the aisle.

Up the aisle. The words froze in her mind.

This was supposed to be the happiest day of her life, yet she felt as if she were embarking on a walk to nowhere. Could she do it? Soon, there would be no turning back. She'd be Charles's wife. By her own standards, that would be for the rest of her life.

Suddenly, she found herself looking down the road to a future filled with Charles. What she saw frightened the stuffing out of her.

Charles, who frowned if she went barefoot and who didn't like the sporty little red cars with cramped back seats. Charles, who left half the strawberry instead of greedily enjoying every succulent drop. Charles, who would never chase her around a lighthouse and smother her with kisses when he caught her.

The music swelled and Lizzie took Katie's arm. They stepped into the doorway leading to the altar. The church overflowed with people. A large, white satin bow marked each row of pews. White mums, pink roses, creamy yellow carnations and deep-green ivy spilled over the sides of baskets on the altar. It looked as if the setting had been pulled from the pages of *Bride* magazine.

Katie's gaze slipped to the man waiting with his back to her. He appeared to be miles away, untouchable. She wanted to reach out for the security he'd always represented. Instead, her mind's eye darted back to the future.

A row of proper little children sat on assigned chairs eating dinner. At the end of the table Charles, his handsome face serious, presided. Neither dinner chatter nor laughter bubbled from them. In unison, they lifted their forks and began eating. Suddenly, one of them laughed. Katie's gaze darted nervously to Charles, but sitting at the end of the table was Grant, his face creased in a playful grin.

Katie closed her eyes to banish the vision, then hesitantly took her first step toward a new life. She opened her eyes and behind the mist of her veil, a new scene took shape in her mind.

Charles leaned to kiss her. She recoiled. She stared at him for a long time, wondering why his kisses didn't entice her. Why his embrace brought her neither security, nor comfort. Then it wasn't Charles. Grant held his arms out to her. But instead of walking into them, she turned away, searching for the safety of Charles. Seeing him, she reached out. Slowly, he faded until nothing remained but insubstantial mist.

The organ music gained volume and broke into her

daydream. The man at the altar shifted nervously from one foot to the other. She could barely see him through the cascade of white lace hanging in front of her face.

Again the visions intruded.

This time, she stood in a deserted little cottage on a small island. Firelight lit the room. Laughter filled the empty corners. Love warmed the couple sprawled in front of the hearth. The remains of strawberries scattered everywhere perfumed the room with their fragrance. Katie held her breath while the man turned his face to the firelight, then tenderly kissed the woman. Grant. But the woman he smiled down at with loving eyes wasn't Katie Donovan.

Grant with someone else. The pain jabbing deep into her heart nearly toppled her. She stumbled.

Her mother clutched at her arm.

"Are you okay?" Lizzie whispered.

Katie nodded. "I think so." But she wasn't okay. She'd never be okay again.

"Just wedding jitters," Lizzie said. She tightened her grip on Katie's arm. "You'll be fine in a few minutes."

Serious doubt as to whether she'd ever be fine again without Grant buffeted Katie's mind.

Dragging her gaze from where Charles waited at the altar, she concentrated on glimpses of the friends, relatives and loved ones who had come to see her happily married. Harriet Biddle smiled back at her, her cheeks damp with tears. Alfred sat beside her, looking at Katie with an odd expression softening his stern features.

Why were they here? Who invited them? Probably Lizzie.

After the fiasco on the island, she'd have thought both of them would have never wanted to lay eyes on her again. Harriet had been so sincere in her efforts to heal a marriage that she saw as worth saving. Even Alfred, in his own way, had tried. How she'd hated deceiving them.

At that moment, she knew that marrying Charles would be nothing more than an extension of that lie. And that's what this entire wedding was—a lie. She'd been deceiving herself and Charles ever since she'd walked away from Grant on Windsor Island.

She couldn't marry Charles. It wouldn't be fair to him or to her. She loved Grant. She'd never stopped and would probably go on loving him for the rest of her life.

Lizzie had been right to go back to Katie's father. Life without the man you love *was* infinitely worse than life with him, even if he wasn't always there. She'd been wrong to turn away from Grant, to try to convince him to give up his dreams. Harriet loved Alfred despite his workaholic ways. Her mother loved her father enough to try repeatedly to find that kind of love again. Why couldn't she love Grant as he was? Was she less of a woman than Harriet and her mother? Did she love Grant any less?

She looked up. Barely a few feet away, Charles waited, his back still turned to her. Regretting having let this wedding go this far, she made up her mind to tell him it could never happen. She would leave here and try to heal her relationship with Grant.

Her head spun as she took the last few steps to bring her even with Charles.

Katie opened her mouth to say the words that would free both of them from making a horrible mistake.

He turned.

Suddenly, she couldn't speak, couldn't breathe.

Her antique lace veil seemed to smother her.

She tried to push it away. Her fingers tangled in the material. Like a moth caught in a spiderweb, she struggled to free herself.

As an even heavier veil of inky blackness washed over her, her strength deserted her. Her knees gave way. She felt herself slipping to the floor.

Chapter Thirteen

"Katie?"

Through a smothering fog, Katie fought to reach the surface. The nightmare she'd been having while walking up the aisle had followed her into this dreamy state she found herself fighting to be free of.

"Katie?"

That couldn't be Grant's voice calling her name and smoothing her cheek with his thumb. He couldn't actually be here. It had been her fevered thoughts that had summoned him. That's why when, at the altar, Charles had turned to her, she'd seen Grant.

"Katie?"

Fate was so unkind to befuddle her mind now. Now, when she had to keep her wits about her long enough to explain to Charles. Now, when a church full of people expected her to get up off this floor and marry a man she cared deeply for, but could never love the way he deserved to be loved. Now, when she needed Grant more than ever before.

"Katie?"

Why wouldn't they just stick a gardenia in her hand

and leave her here to die on her bed of antique lace and silk in peaceful humiliation?

"Kathleen?"

Charles. At last, sanity had returned.

Slowly, she opened her eyes. Not just Charles, not just Grant, but both of them stared down at her.

She blinked.

They were still there.

She squeezed her eyes closed again, then slowly opened first one, then the other. Over Grant's shoulder, in a matching tux, Charles studied her with a concerned expression. But her gaze locked on Grant.

"So, you decided to come back to me." Grant smiled, but inside he was trying hard to swallow the panic that had risen when Katie passed out at his feet.

She blinked. Her gaze darted from him to Charles. "You knew?"

"Knew what?" Charles asked the question from over Grant's shoulder.

"What I was thinking—" Katie struggled to a sitting position on the minister's living room couch, then shook her head. "Never mind."

Feeling like a new member of the Three Stooges and totally out of the loop, Grant moved to the side to make room for the layers of antique lace surrounding Katie.

Gads, but the woman is beautiful. That gown makes her look like a Dresden doll.

"How are you feeling?" Lizzie ran her hand over Katie's forehead.

"Like I just swam the Atlantic Ocean during a hurricane." Katie scanned the room.

Harriet and Alfred stared at her from near a large bay window. Grant could tell by Katie's wide-eyed expression that she was wondering what they were doing there. It was time for an explanation. He should have known better than to let Charles, Harriet and Lizzie talk him into surprising Katie at the altar. His only excuse was that he loved Katie and hell could have frozen over before he'd have missed this last chance to make things right between them.

Grant cleared his throat. "Katie, we need to talk."

Groaning, Katie rested her forehead in her hand. "Every time you say that, problems follow."

Hopefully, she was wrong about that this time. Hopefully the only problem to be solved would be where they'd spend their honeymoon.

"I think, Grant, since Harriet and I were the ones who originally cooked up this plan, that I should make the explanations." Charles stepped around him.

Kneeling in front of Katie, he gently hooked his forefinger under her chin and raised it.

"Back on the island, when I saw you with Grant, it occurred to me that you might have been hiding behind our relationship to avoid confronting your love for Grant." When she opened her mouth to speak, Charles moved his finger to seal her lips. "Let me finish. You never looked at me the way you did Grant. Your love radiated from your eyes."

Katie cast a side glance at Grant. Her love for him

shone from their green depths, just like Charles said, just like it had that night on Little Windsor.

"But it wasn't until, when Alfred announced that your marriage wasn't legal and I saw the disappointment register in them that I knew for sure if you married me, you'd have been settling for second best." He took her hand and laid it in Grant's. "This is the man you should be marrying, not me."

Grant closed his fingers around her hand and was rewarded with a returned squeeze. His heart filled and his hopes soared.

"When I spoke to Harriet about it, she agreed and that's when we began planning this. Maybe it was crazy. Maybe not. All I knew was that somehow, I had to make you see who it was you truly loved."

In his mind, Grant hoped that he was half the man Charles was proving to be. In his heart, he hoped Katie was listening.

Katie touched Charles's face with her free hand. "You'll never know how sorry I am that I put you through this."

"Please, don't be sorry. I also realized that I would have been shortchanging myself if I'd let you go through with the wedding, so there was a bit of self-ishness involved here. I want a woman who will look at me the way you look at Grant. And I want to feel the depth of emotion from that look that Grant does. I refuse to settle for any less. You showed me that."

Charles leaned forward and kissed Katie's cheek, then stood. "Be happy, Kathleen." He stepped back and looked at Grant. "Take care of her. She's very special."

"I know that now." He extended his hand to Charles. "Thanks. We owe you for this."

Waving his hand as if dismissing Grant's words, Charles turned to the others in the room. "I assume these two have a lot of talking to do and we should leave them to it." Like a shepherd, he ushered the others from the room.

Just before he closed the door behind them, he leaned back through the opening. "By the way, there's a marriage license waiting for your signatures on the desk over there. Make sure you sign it. We don't want any questions this time." The door started to swing closed, then opened again. "And get a move on. We have a bunch of wedding guests waiting for the ceremony to start." He smiled at them and closed the door.

An awkward silence filled the empty room. Grant knew he had things to say to Katie, but he didn't know where to start, especially with her hand resting trustingly in his.

"Katie, I—"

Katie stopped his words with her mouth. Grant could have objected, he could have insisted that they talk, but talking was far from the thoughts racing through his mind. Instead, he drew Katie, *his Katie,* into his arms and kissed her back with all the love his heart held.

"Let's get this thing legalized before something else comes up," Katie murmured against his lips.

Smiling, Grant pulled her hard against him, imprinting her with the lower half of his body. "Something already has."

Laughing, they signed the papers, then walked from the room, their arms around each other. As they left, Grant glanced over his shoulder. Next to the couch rested Katie's white satin high heels. His Katie was back, this time for good.

THE SMELL OF wild strawberries drifted to Katie. Seconds later something soft and velvety caressed her cheek. Blinking against the sudden brightness of the sun, she opened her eyes. Leaning over her, holding a strawberry in one hand and a wild pink rugose rose in the other, was her husband of two days.

"Are you going to spend our entire honeymoon sleeping, Mrs. Waverly?"

Grinning, Katie threw her arms around his neck and pulled his lips to hers for a quick kiss. "And what are these treasures you bring to me?"

"Bribes." He kissed her neck, right where the pulse pounded out the beat of her aroused heart.

"Bribes for what?"

"Ravaging your body." He growled out the words, then nipped her earlobe playfully. "These may be the most elaborate gifts I'll be able to shower you with for a while."

The reminder of all Grant had given up sobered Katie. "Are you sure you want to leave Alfred's firm? I don't want you giving it up for some twisted idea I had of what a husband should be."

"I'm sure." Grant sat and brought his knees up under his chin.

Katie followed suit. Crossing her forearms over her knees, she stared at the waves breaking on the jagged rocks a few feet away. The smell of salt water and strawberries evoked memories of their last visit to Little Windsor.

In the interim, Harriet had managed to get Elmer to fix up the little cottage and move enough furniture in to make it very hospitable and homey. He'd even laid in a supply of wood for the fireplace, added a generator and an old refrigerator and filled it with, among other things, two very large, cooked lobsters for their first dinner as man and wife.

"You won't miss the success you had at Alfred's law offices?" Katie needed to know that Grant's choice of changes in his career were for him and not her. Only then could he be happy with his new job.

"I won't miss it. I had the mistaken idea that money was everything, that without it, a person couldn't find happiness."

"And now?"

He turned to her, then pressed her back into the sea grass. "And now, I know that the only thing I need to make me happy is to roll over in bed in the morning and find you lying beside me. To look up from my plate at dinner and find you across the table. To come home from a long day and walk into your arms." He kissed her eyes. "To know that when my heart aches, you'll be there to apply the first aid."

He kissed her hard and long. When he pulled away, Katie was fighting for her breath.

"I love you, my Katie. I never stopped. And when I thought I'd lost you again, I learned the true value of life."

Over his shoulder, Katie could see the evening star just coming to life in the darkening sky. She closed her eyes and wished. She wished for her mother to find happiness again, alone or with another man who could bring to life in her the kind of love that Katie felt for Grant. She wished for Charles to find that woman who would make his heart sing the way hers was right now. She wished that she would never again take Grant's dreams from him or consider them trivial in comparison to hers.

"What are you thinking?" Grant shifted his weight to cover her.

"I wasn't thinking. I was wishing on the evening star."

"Did you make a wish for me?"

Katie smiled. "I made a wish for us."

Grant's mouth took hers, and she forgot about stars and wishes and concentrated on the man she loved. Her thoughts spiraled out of sight of the small island on which they were honeymooning. They soared far into the future and beyond to the time when she and Grant would have babies and grow old together.

"I love you," she said, when they'd pulled apart. Her eyes repeated her declaration.

He could feel Katie's love spreading through him, warming him and securing him. Grant had needed that for so long. Only his Katie had the power to lift him to the heavens with those three words that opened her heart to him.

This was the love he'd forgotten. The kind that wraps you in its embrace and makes life the joy it should be. The kind that no amount of money can buy.

Katie shivered.

"Cold?"

She nodded and snuggled deeper into his embrace. "A little."

"Let's go back to the cottage."

"Is this where you ravage my body?" she asked in a deep sultry voice.

He loved it when she was like this, playful and sexy as hell. "Katie, promise me something."

She kissed him. "Anything."

"Promise you'll never become that starched woman I met in St. Augustine again. You were so brittle and proper. Nothing like the woman who taught me to eat strawberries."

Katie grinned up at him. Behind him, she reached in the picnic basket. "Have I ever shown you—" she brought her arm around between them and brandished a piece of fruit "—the art of eating a banana?"

HARLEQUIN®
AMERICAN ◆ ROMANCE®

*They're handsome, they're sexy, they're
determined to remain single.
But these two "bachelors" are about to
receive the shock of their lives...*

OOPS! STILL MARRIED!

**August 1999—#787 THE OVERNIGHT GROOM
by Elizabeth Sinclair**
Grant Waverly must persuade Katie Donovan to
continue their newly discovered marriage for just two
more intimate weeks....

**September 1999—#790 OVERNIGHT FATHER
by Debbi Rawlins**
Matthew Monroe never forgot the woman he'd once
married for convenience. And now Lexy Monroe
needs the man from whom she's kept
one little secret....

Look for the special *Oops! Still Married!*
duet, coming to you soon—only from
Harlequin American Romance®!

The honeymoon is just beginning...

Available at your favorite retail outlet.

HARLEQUIN®
Makes any time special ™

Celebrate **15** years with

 **HARLEQUIN®**
Makes any time special ™

 WIN A DREAM

In celebration of Harlequin®'s golden anniversary

Enter to win a *dream!* You could win:

- A luxurious trip for two to *The Renaissance Cottonwoods Resort* in Scottsdale, Arizona, or

- A bouquet of flowers once a week for a year from **FTD**, or

- A $500 shopping spree, or

- A fabulous bath & body gift basket, including **K-tel's** *Candlelight and Romance* 5-CD set.

Look for **WIN A DREAM** flash on specially marked Harlequin® titles by Penny Jordan, Dallas Schulze, Anne Stuart and Kristine Rolofson in October 1999*.

 FTD

RENAISSANCE. COTTONWOODS RESORT SCOTTSDALE, ARIZONA

 K·TEL

"Fascinating—you'll want to take
this home!"
—Marie Ferrarella

"Each page is filled with a brand-new
surprise."
—Suzanne Brockmann

"Makes reading a new and joyous
experience all over again."
—Tara Taylor Quinn

See what all your favorite authors
are talking about.

Coming October 1999 to a retail store near you.

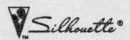